HARLEQUIN®
Presents

Happy New Year! Have you made any resolutions for 2007?

The editors of Harlequin Presents books have made their resolution: to continue doing their very best to bring you the ultimate in emotional excitement every month during the coming year—stories that totally deliver on compelling characters, dramatic story lines, fabulous foreign settings, intense feelings and sizzling sensuality!

January gets us off to a good start with the best selection of international heroes—two Italian playboys, two gorgeous Greek tycoons, a French count, a debonair Brit, a passionate Spaniard and a handsome Aussie. Yummy!

We also have the crème de la crème of authors from around the world: Michelle Reid, Trish Morey, Sarah Morgan, Melanie Milburne, Sara Craven, Margaret Mayo, Helen Brooks and Annie West, who debuts with her very first novel, *A Mistress for the Taking*.

Join us again next month for more of your favorites, including Penny Jordan, Lucy Monroe and Carole Mortimer—seduction and passion are guaranteed!

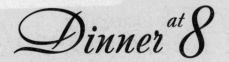

Helen Brooks

THE MILLIONAIRE'S PROSPECTIVE WIFE

Dinner at 8

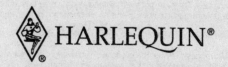

HARLEQUIN®

TORONTO • NEW YORK • LONDON
AMSTERDAM • PARIS • SYDNEY • HAMBURG
STOCKHOLM • ATHENS • TOKYO • MILAN • MADRID
PRAGUE • WARSAW • BUDAPEST • AUCKLAND

ISBN-13: 978-0-373-12601-9
ISBN-10:   0-373-12601-8

THE MILLIONAIRE'S PROSPECTIVE WIFE

First North American Publication 2007.

Copyright © 2005 by Helen Brooks.

www.eHarlequin.com

Printed in U.S.A.

All about the author...
Helen Brooks

HELEN BROOKS was born and educated in
Northampton, England. She met her husband at the age
of sixteen and thirty-five years later the magic is still
there. They have three lovely children and a menagerie
of animals in the house! The children, friends and pets
all keep the house buzzing and the food cupboards
empty, but Helen wouldn't have it any other way.

Helen began writing in 1990 as she approached
that milestone of a birthday—forty! She realized her
two teenage ambitions (writing a novel and learning
to drive) had been lost amid babies and family life,
so she set about resurrecting them. Her first novel
was accepted after one rewrite, and she passed her
driving test (the former was a joy and the latter an
unmitigated nightmare).

Helen's a committed Christian and fervent animal lover.
She finds time is always at a premium, but somehow
fits in walks in the countryside with her husband and
dogs, meals out followed by the cinema or theater,
reading, swimming and visiting with friends. She also
enjoys sitting in her wonderfully therapeutic, rambling
old garden in the sun with a glass of red wine, (under
the guise of resting while thinking, of course!).

Since becoming a full-time writer, Helen has found
her occupation to be one of pure joy. She loves
exploring what makes people tick and finds the old
adage "truth is stranger than fiction" to be absolutely
true. She would love to hear from any readers,
care of Harlequin Presents.

CHAPTER ONE

THE moment Cory let Rufus off the lead she knew it was a big mistake. The powerful Labrador cross golden retriever shot across Hyde Park like a bat out of hell, mothers whisking toddlers up into their arms at his approach and elderly couples leaping out of his way with a nimbleness they probably thought had been lost to them years before. Even the group of young people who had been ambling towards them clad in strategically slashed jeans and with piercings in seemingly every nook and cranny lost their cool aplomb, scattering with shrieks and cries which—on the whole, Cory was thankful to note—were good-humoured.

For the first minute or so of following in the dog's wake Cory shouted apologies to all and sundry, then, when Rufus showed no signs of slowing down, she kept her breath for running.

Why hadn't she listened to her aunt? Cory silently berated herself as she panted after the dog, wasting valuable breath every twenty yards or so by screeching his name. But Rufus had been so docile and obliging on the walk down Bayswater Road from her aunt's house, sitting at all the right times without being told and keeping to heel like an old pro. And the deep brown eyes had been so imploring once they'd entered the park, the doggy expression of longing as he'd watched other canines chasing balls and playing making her feel like the wicked witch of the west.

'Keep him on the lead, Cory,' Aunt Joan had warned as she'd seen them off at the door, her left leg encased in plaster due to a nasty fall a couple of weeks before. 'I can

7

just about trust him to come back now but I don't know how he would react with someone else. He's perfectly friendly, of course, and just adores children and other dogs, but the original owners kept him confined all the time as well as neglecting him in other ways, as you know. The poor darling.'

'The poor darling' was not the phrase she'd choose to describe the dog right at this moment, Cory thought grimly. Her lungs felt as though they were going to burst and her throat and chest were on fire. There were various choice names which sprang to mind but poor and darling didn't feature in any of them.

Rufus having made a couple of lightning stops to sniff the certain part of other canines' anatomies which dogs found so interesting, Cory now found herself closer to him than at any time since the undignified chase had begun. Summoning all her strength, she bellowed, *'Rufus! Stay!'* just as the animal prepared to take off from socialising with a French poodle. The golden head turned, brown eyes considering her with a faintly amazed expression as though he couldn't understand why she wasn't entering wholeheartedly into this wonderful game he'd organised. Seizing the opportunity, Cory growled, *'Come here. Heel, Rufus.'*

There was still a good fifty yards between them but she couldn't run any more, the stitch in her side excruciating. Whether it was her ferocious voice or the fact that she had slowed down to a walk, Cory didn't know, but the big dog suddenly seemed to realise all was not well. After one more moment of hesitation he took off again, but this time headed straight for her, determined to impress her by the speed with which he obeyed. It was doubtful he even noticed the tall, well-dressed figure about to cross his path. There was one endless moment when man and dog met and then five or six stone of sheer canine muscle sent the unfortunate figure hurtling into the air.

A very nice leather briefcase went one way, the suit jacket which had been slung over one shirt-clad arm another, and all Cory could do was to look in unmitigated horror. The man landed on his back with earth-shaking force and even Rufus realised he'd committed a *faux pas*. He was slinking obsequiously around the prostrate figure on the grass when Cory reached them, his ears flat to his face and his floppy jowls shaking as though he was about to burst into tears.

'Oh, I'm sorry, I'm so, so sorry.' Cory went down on to her knees in a flurry of blue denim jeans, pink shirt and tumbled hair the colour of rich dark chocolate. 'Are you all right?'

The man remained perfectly still for another moment and then drew air into his body with something of a tortured groan. It probably wasn't the moment to notice it was an exceptionally fit body—tall, lean and muscled with an aggressive masculinity that was rawly sexy—or that the jet-black hair topped a face that was out-and-out dynamite.

Cory swallowed. Pierce Brosnan, Orlando Bloom, Brad Pitt—eat your hearts out. She had to swallow again before she could say, 'Have you broken anything?'

A pair of very blue eyes met hers. In spite of his prone position and the fact he'd had all the air knocked out of him—or maybe because of it—they were lethal, the one rapier sharp glance saying more than mere words could ever have done. When Cory went to help him as he sat up he motioned her hands away with a cutting action that was savage. It was unfortunate Rufus chose that moment to make his apology by means of a long slobbery lick across one chiselled cheekbone. The man froze for a second but still didn't say a word before he rose to his feet.

He was tall. Cory found herself looking up some distance as she too stood up. Very tall. And angry. Very, very angry.

'Is it yours?'

'I'm sorry.' She was still frozen by the icy eyes and the way the set of his hard mouth gave the handsome face a harsh cast, and her brain wasn't working properly.

'That.' He gestured furiously in Rufus's direction. 'Is it—? Hell!' The original sentence was cut off. 'What's he eating?'

Oh, no. Please, no. This couldn't be happening. She took the mobile phone out of Rufus's wet jaws but the damage was already done. Neither of them had noticed the dog snuffling in the discarded jacket. 'Was...was it expensive?' she asked in a small voice whilst already knowing the answer. It was a state of the art, super dooper technological miracle of a phone. What else? But it hadn't been designed to withstand the power of those big jaws.

He ignored the outstretched hand with the chewed phone and took a deep breath, retrieving his briefcase and jacket and wincing slightly as he did so.

He *was* hurt. But then of course he would be. Meeting an express train in the middle of Hyde Park on a Saturday morning was something even Superman would have found a little hard to take. 'I'm sorry,' she said again. 'I shouldn't have taken him off the lead.'

Dark eyebrows climbed sardonically. 'Really?'

He wasn't being very gracious but she supposed she couldn't blame him. Cory took a deep breath. 'I'll pay for any damage, of course,' she said with a little upward jerk of her chin which wasn't lost on the man in front of her. 'To the phone, your suit...anything,' she finished lamely.

The eyebrows went a touch higher. 'Am I supposed to say thank you here?' he drawled silkily.

What a thoroughly unpleasant individual. Cory found she

could ignore the beauty of the sky-blue eyes quite well now. It wasn't so much what he said but the way that he said it which was so nasty. 'Not at all,' she said curtly, her whole body stiffening. 'I'm merely making the point, that's all.'

Rufus had seated himself at the man's side as though he had disowned her and was now looking the very picture of docility, his big head moving interestedly from one to the other as they had spoken. Cory found she could have throttled him. Preparing to clip the lead back on his collar, she said, 'Rufus, come here,' just as the flirtatious French poodle the dog had been eyeing up earlier sauntered past.

Her despairing, 'Rufus, *no*!' was lost as he sprang up, blind and deaf to anything but his hormones.

He had only gone a few feet when one bitingly sharp, deep 'Sit!' brought him skidding into the required position seemingly in mid-air. *'Heel,'* followed with equal success, the dog performing a perfect Crufts manoeuvre to arrive in ingratiatingly quick time pressed close against the man's legs. As an authoritative male hand stretched out for the lead Cory handed it over. The next moment both lead and dog were returned to her.

'Thank you.' It was said with extreme reluctance.

'You can't suggest he does what he's told,' the man said with irritating coolness. 'It's all in the tone.'

'You're an expert on dogs?' Cory responded before she could stop herself.

'No.' In a leisurely exercise which stopped just short of being insulting, heavily lashed blue eyes wandered over her hot face. 'I'm an expert on being obeyed.'

Somehow she didn't doubt that.

'Obedience classes would be good for you,' he continued with insufferable condescension.

It didn't escape her notice that he had said good for her

rather than the dog. The fact that he had several bits of grass in his perfectly groomed hair gave her savage satisfaction. 'He's not mine,' she said shortly. 'My aunt recently acquired him from a dog sanctuary. They thought he'd been locked away in a shed from when he was a puppy and just thrown scraps now and again. She *has* been taking him to classes—' it was wonderful to be able to say it in all truth '—but she's broken her leg and so I offered to give him a walk this morning.'

The sapphire gaze left her face and turned downwards to the golden dog. 'Poor old boy,' he said directly to Rufus who wagged his tail furiously.

And then his voice lost the brief softness and returned to its former coldness when he looked at her again and said, 'For the sake of the dog and not least anyone in his path, keep him on the lead while your aunt is indisposed, would you?'

She bit her lip hard to prevent the spate of words which sprang to mind and counted to ten. 'I'd worked that one out for myself.'

'Good.'

It looked as though he was going to walk away and now Cory said quickly, 'Your phone; I meant what I said about paying for a new one. Do you want my telephone number and address?'

He raised his brow. 'Are you always so exceedingly generous in giving complete strangers your private details?'

He was deliberately needling her and she recognised it but still couldn't help being caught on the raw. 'I'm not in charge of a dog which knocks people down every day,' she returned smartly.

He muttered something she thought might be, 'Thank heaven for small mercies,' before saying, 'Don't worry about the phone, Ms…?'

'James. Cory James.' She looked at him steadily through velvet-brown eyes just a shade or two lighter than her hair. 'And I insist on paying for a new one, Mr...?'

'My name is Nick Morgan and, I repeat, forget about the phone.' He now took it from her, pocketing it nonchalantly.

'I can't do that.' The obstinate streak which ran through her slender frame like a rod of steel came into play. 'Rufus has ruined it and I wouldn't feel happy unless I make amends.'

The square male jaw tightened. 'It's not necessary.'

'*I* feel it is.'

'Are you always this—' he hesitated for the merest fraction of a second, and when he finished '—determined?' she felt sure that was not what he'd been about to say.

'Always.' She didn't smile and neither did he.

He folded his arms, surveying her for some moments without speaking. He was standing a couple of feet from her and in spite of herself her pulse was racing. It was his overwhelming masculinity that was sending the blood coursing, she told herself irritably, and she hated that he could affect her so. It wasn't attraction—it definitely, *definitely* wasn't attraction, she reiterated as though someone had challenged her on it—but more an awareness of the you Tarzan, me Jane type of definition of the sexes. What with his height, which must be at least six-three or four, and the hard look to his body, he was...well...

She couldn't find a word to describe what Nick Morgan was and so she gave up the struggle as he spoke again.

'A new phone will be provided the moment I walk into my offices,' he said evenly, 'but if you really feel the need for atonement?'

'I do.'

A thin smile curved across his mouth as though he found something amusing. The next moment Cory realised it was her reaction to his next words he had been anticipating with relish. 'Then I need a partner for a social occasion tonight and my proposed date has had to fly out to New York at short notice.' His eyes pierced her with laser brightness. 'Care to oblige?'

Cory took a moment to compose herself. She had never been so taken aback in her life. Was he joking?

Her face must have reflected her thoughts because the smile widened. 'I'm quite serious. Of course, if you have a previous engagement or a husband or boyfriend who might object…' He let his voice trail away but his gaze never left her.

She could lie. No, no she couldn't, she corrected herself in the next instant, because he'd know. Somehow she knew without question that he would be able to discern any fabrication a mile off. She looked at him squarely. 'I'm not in a relationship,' she said shortly. 'What exactly is involved tonight?'

'Cocktails, dinner, dancing.'

It wasn't a proper explanation and they both knew it. Cory waited for more.

After a few seconds had stretched themselves into what was to Cory unbearable tension, he said, 'I've recently taken over a particular company and this is a goodwill gesture by me for the senior management and their partners. Nothing heavy, you know? Merely a table at Templegate and us all getting to know each other on a social level.'

Cory stared at him, her mind buzzing behind the steady brown of her eyes. A table at Templegate for the evening? That was going to cost him an arm and a leg. She had never had the opportunity to see inside the most famous nightclub in London herself, but it was where the young, rich and beautiful went to see and be seen. Trendy magazines were always brimming with pictures of this or that celebrity dancing the night away there and it was common knowledge that dinner equated to a second mortgage. She swallowed hard. 'A party of how many?' she asked with what she considered commendable matter-of-factness.

'Just sixteen, or fifteen as of eight o'clock this morning,' he added wryly. 'My date was offered a modelling assignment she apparently couldn't refuse.'

His girlfriend was a model? But of course she was— what else? Cory asked herself waspishly. He was obviously filthy rich and enormously successful—if the takeover remark was anything to go by. That, added to his good looks, would make him the catch of the year and ensure women were lining up in their droves. This last thought caused her to say, 'But you must have someone else you can ask to stand in?'

'Must I?' he countered with lazy amusement.

'Well, haven't you?'

He didn't answer this directly. What he did say was, 'You wanted to make reparation for the dog and I suggested a way you could do so. If it's not to your liking, that's fine.'

It wasn't to her liking! Of *course* it wasn't to her liking. The kind of women who put in an appearance at Templegate wouldn't be seen dead in anything other than Versace or Gabbana or Armani; the shoes that clad their tiny feet would take a couple of months of her wages alone. And to spend the evening in the company of this complete stranger who was entertaining other complete strangers would be torture. She'd be terrified of saying or doing something wrong for a start, and what if they were all snooty and standoffish or just plain uncommunicative?

She took one swift glance around the park, which was bathed in warm June sunlight, as though it was going to help her before bringing her eyes back to the keen blue gaze. 'All right,' she heard herself saying with faint disbelief. 'If that's what you want, fine, although I'd rather just pay for the phone and be done with it.'

'Not the most gracious acceptance to dinner I've ever received.' The amusement was still very much in evidence as he reached into his briefcase and extracted a small gold-embossed card which he handed to her.

Cory glanced down expecting a formal business card, but it merely stated his name followed by four telephone numbers.

'Forget the first number, that's my home in Barnstaple,' he said a touch impatiently. 'The second is my London flat and the third my private line at the office. Obviously the mobile number is a little irrelevant now.' Piercing blue eyes fastened on Rufus for a moment and the big dog shifted guiltily at her feet. Nick's mouth twitched and then he glanced at the gold wrist-watch on one tanned wrist, his brow furrowing and the impatience more pronounced as he said, 'I'm late for an important meeting, Miss James. Ring the flat after six tonight to give me your address, or the office number if you need me before that. The table's booked for eight-thirty, incidentally, but we're meeting in the cocktail bar at eight. I would like to be at the club no later than seven-thirty. Is that acceptable to you?'

The vivid blue eyes raked her face again and her pulse gave an unexplained jump. She managed a nod while she took a deep breath. 'Look, I'm just an ordinary working girl,' she said a little breathlessly. 'I'm not used to places like Templegate, to be frank. If you find someone more suitable today who can help you then feel free to tell me tonight when I phone. I'll quite understand.'

He had been about to walk away but now he turned and looked at her. There was a swift assessment when his gaze moved over her from the top of her head to the soles of her trainers. His expression didn't alter and neither did the tone of his voice change when he said, 'I shan't change my mind, Miss James. Goodbye.'

Well! Cory's face was burning as she watched him walk away with long strides which soon put him far into the distance. He'd looked at her as if she was a horse he was considering buying!

She stood for a few moments more until a whine at her feet brought her out of the maelstrom of her thoughts. Glancing down at Rufus she saw he had the nerve to be looking hard done by at the inactivity. 'Don't even go there,' she warned him fiercely. 'This is all your fault.'

The dog grinned back at her before leaping to his feet and straining at the leash, his nose twitching as a cute Bearded Collie with a topknot tied with a big pink bow to keep the hair out of her eyes swayed past, a definite come-hither wiggle to her silky rear end.

'You definitely need a certain little operation, if you ask me,' Cory grumbled, before raising her eyes to gaze into the distance again. Blow, he'd gone. She shaded her eyes against the glare of the sun but after a moment or two was forced to accept he had disappeared from view.

All around the normal Saturday scenario was taking place—kids skateboarding, families strolling, couples stretched out on the grass sunbathing or reading, folk walking their dogs, groups of teenagers playing football or cricket or throwing Frisbees to each other—but she felt suddenly separate from it all. A run-of-the-mill walk in the park had suddenly turned into something extraordinary and, now he had gone, she had time to actually consider what had happened and she felt panic rise hot and strong.

She must be mad—stark staring mad—to agree to accompany him to Templegate tonight! Not just accompany him but virtually act as hostess to a group of people she'd

never seen before in her life. Why hadn't she said no? Why
hadn't she taken the get-out clause he'd offered? What on
earth had prompted her to acquiesce to such a ridiculous
proposition?

She brushed the memory of a striking, evenly planed face
and steel-hard body out of her mind determinedly. It wasn't
him as a person, she told herself firmly as she began to
continue the walk round the park. She wasn't interested in
Nick Morgan, not in the least. That would be sheer madness. Anyway, he already had a girlfriend and the last thing
she was looking for was a relationship of any kind. No,
she'd felt obliged to make amends, that was all.

She glanced down at Rufus trotting happily at her side
and groaned inwardly. Why had she let him off the lead?
Aunt Joan had been specific and she'd ignored her advice—
and not for the first time in her life, she added miserably.
But she wasn't going to think of William Patterson now.
She had enough problems right at this moment as it was,
the most immediate being—what was she going to wear
tonight? She would have to do some emergency shopping
because she hadn't got a thing that would pass in
Templegate's fabled surroundings.

As her feet quickened in time with the swirly butterflies
in her stomach, Rufus had the most energetic walk he'd
had for some time, and by the time the pair of them reached
Cory's aunt's house they were both panting.

'Are you all right, dear?' her aunt asked mildly as she
opened the door. 'You look a little warm.'

Warm would be great. Just being over-warm would be
heaven right now. 'I did a silly thing,' Cory said miserably
as she stepped into the cool hall. 'A very silly thing as it's
turned out.'

'Really?'

She nodded.

'Ooh, lovely,' her aunt said happily. 'I'm always doing silly things and it's so reassuring when someone as together as you does too. The coffee pot's on, come and tell me all about it.'

Rufus settled in his basket, gnawing frenziedly at an enormous hide bone, and with a mug of fragrant coffee and a plate of chocolate digestives in front of her Cory felt a little better as she related the events of the morning. There was something terribly homely and nice in sitting in her aunt's farmhouse-type kitchen with a dog at their feet and bright sunlight picking the colour out of a bunch of marigolds in a vase on the windowsill.

When she'd finished explaining, her aunt was beaming. 'But that's wonderful,' she said enthusiastically. 'You'll have a wonderful meal in the most wonderful place and this man sounds—'

'Wonderful?' Cory interrupted wryly. There had been a sight too many wonderfuls as far as she was concerned. She was terrified, and here was her aunt acting as though she had just won the lottery or something.

'I was going to say very reasonable,' her aunt said reproachfully. 'He could have shouted or caused a fuss after all. Lots of people *would* have, and in this day and age of everyone suing everyone else at the drop of a hat...' She sighed, wagging her head in despair at the current trend. 'And all this Mr Morgan did was to ask you out to dinner at the most fabulous place. I mean, what's the problem?'

Put like that there wasn't one, but then her aunt hadn't seen Nick Morgan. Cory swallowed hard. 'I don't have a thing to wear,' she prevaricated, but even to her own ears it sounded weak. 'Not something that carries a million dollar label anyway.'

'Is that all?' The complacency was now most certainly of the Cheshire cat variety as Joan's smile widened. 'Darling go and see a friend of mine, Chantal Lemoine of Mayfair. She'll fix you up.'

This wasn't comforting. Cory loved her aunt—since her parents had died within a year of each other when she had been at university, her aunt was the only close relative she had—but Joan had never married and had made her career her life before she'd retired early at the age of fifty after a heart attack scare. She'd had a high-powered position in the world of fashion and hadn't thought anything of spending an exorbitant amount on a simple skirt or top. Since leaving university four years ago Cory, on the other hand, had felt drawn to work in the sector of social care, something which involved long hours, stress and a merely adequate salary. A salary which didn't lend itself to designer establishments.

Whether her aunt sensed what she was thinking Cory wasn't sure, but the next moment the older woman had picked up the telephone saying, 'I'm ringing Chantal, all right? It's your birthday in a few weeks' time and I didn't have a clue what to get you. This is the perfect answer. You go and choose something absolutely outrageously expensive. You've been an angel to me since my fall and I want to thank you.'

'I couldn't, Aunty.' Cory's cheeks were pink.

'You could and will.' And then Joan's expression and voice changed as she said softly, putting her hand on Cory's arm, 'Please, darling. For me. You're the daughter I never had and you never let me spoil you. Just this once indulge me, eh?'

Cory wriggled uncomfortably. It was true she looked on her aunt more as a mother than anything else. In spite of being an only child she hadn't been close to either of her parents, who had been so wrapped up in each other they hadn't needed anyone else, not even their daughter. It had been a lonely and not particularly happy childhood in many respects, and her Aunt Joan had often been an oasis in the desert. Whether because of her childhood or perhaps just the way she was made, she'd always been reserved and independent, preferring to help rather than be helped and to give rather than receive.

'Hello, could I speak to Miss Lemoine, please?' Her aunt had taken her hesitation as a yes. When Cory went to speak Joan waved her to silence with a raised hand. 'Chantal? Darling, how are you? It's Joan.' A few seconds and then, 'Yes, we must as soon as this wretched leg of mine is better. Perhaps lunch at Roberto's? Look, the reason I'm calling is to ask a favour. I'm sending Cory to you—you remember she's my niece? She has a very special occasion tonight—at Templegate. Yes, I know, it's very exciting. The thing is, she needs something really gorgeous and I thought you might be able to help. Could you see to her personally? Advise her on what suits her best? I'd come myself but with this leg... Oh, you're a sweetheart. Two o'clock will be fine. Thanks so much, darling. And put it on my account, would you, this is a little birthday treat. Bye-bye, Chantal.'

The receiver replaced, her aunt beamed at her. 'That's settled then. Sweetheart, you're going to have a perfectly lovely time and you'll look beautiful. Chantal will guarantee it.'

Cory smiled but said nothing. The day wasn't going at all as she had planned.

CHAPTER TWO

IT WAS five to seven and Cory was panicking big time, not least because she barely recognized the girl staring back at her out of the mirror. When she'd left Chantal earlier that afternoon, the little Frenchwoman's parting encouragement had been, '*Chérie*, make up your mind to enjoy a night on the tiles in haute couture style! Yes? You will look enchanting. As the late Gianni Versace once said: "If you make an entrance and nobody turns to look at you, my dear, find a back door and leave. And then find a new dress." I promise you, *chérie*, you will not have to find the door,' Chantal had said with great satisfaction. 'Not in that dress.'

It *was* beautiful. Cory's gaze left the frightened eyes in the mirror and travelled downwards. And in this case the clothes did definitely maketh the woman. The midnight-blue silk just missed being black, the cap-sleeved bodice with flattering collar-bone-skimming neckline topping a skirt with the same leaf transparencies and beading, and, as if all that wasn't enough to catch the eye, the skirt had vertiginous side slits. These had caused Cory to protest that she couldn't possibly wear the dress out before she had tried it on, but once Chantal had zipped her up she'd had to admit that it did something to her figure and skin that was riveting.

'This is the one,' the little Frenchwoman had cried. 'This is the dress that makes you a goddess.'

Goddess was going a bit far, Cory thought, her gaze returning to check her make-up for the umpteenth time. But the dress did do something for her that was amazing. She dreaded to think how much it had cost her aunt. None of the clothes in the exclusive shop had had anything so vulgar as a price label. Presumably if one couldn't take the heat one stayed out of the kitchen!

When she'd made noises about the cost, Chantal had merely tapped the side of her small nose and shook her beautifully coiffured head in disapproval. 'This is the gift, yes?' she had scolded, making Cory feel terribly unsophisticated. 'Your aunt will know and this is enough. Now...' She had gone on to recommend another couple of establishments where Cory could purchase suitable accessories but, although she'd thanked the older woman, Cory had known she wouldn't be stepping through their doors. Shoes and bags at several hundred pounds a go just wasn't an option on her salary.

Instead she had looked round various high street shops and market stalls, eventually finding delicate strappy sandals in just the right shade with a little purse to match in Covent Garden. Racing home to her flat in Notting Hill— the purchase of which had taken every last penny of her inheritance, but which had been supremely worth it—she had showered, washed her hair and set about moisturising and perfuming for the night ahead.

Should she have left her hair down? She glanced again at the silky smooth chignon she'd persuaded her shoulder-length waves into. It had seemed too fussy somehow, the dress being so stunning, but her hair had been up and down three times before she had made up her mind.

'Stop it.' She breathed the words out loud into the quiet, pastel-coloured bedroom. 'It's just a nightclub, they're just people like everyone else, *he's* just a man.' And he'd reduced her to talking to herself already after one brief meeting!

An authoritative buzz from the lobby entry intercom

brought her hand to her throat before she breathed deeply, willing the panic to subside. Walking through into the small square hall she steeled herself to press the button situated to the side of her front door. 'Yes, who is it?' she asked with a breathlessness she could have kicked herself for.

'Nick Morgan.' Succinct and to the point.

'I'll be right down, Mr Morgan. If you'd care to wait in the lobby…' She pressed the building's door release before flying back into the bedroom in a tottering scramble which warned her that the sandals didn't lend themselves to anything other than dignified sedateness, not unless she wanted to end up on her rear end, that was. And that was unthinkable in front of Nick Morgan.

Snatching up her purse, which was just large enough to hold her keys, lipstick, two twenty pound notes for emergencies—in case he didn't intend to see her home for example—and a few tissues, she walked carefully back to the hall, opening her front door and then making her way down the wide staircase which led to the lobby.

The old Victorian house had been converted to three fairly large flats, one on each floor. The ground floor flat was owned by a retired couple with a massive German Shepherd called Arnie who had a howl like a wolf's. This was the biggest apartment, having three bedrooms and its own tiny garden. Cory's flat and the one above each had two bedrooms and a large balcony off the sitting room French windows. The young married couple above her had made their balcony into a miniature garden, but Cory's contained a small table and two chairs and a large lacy palm in a big pot and that was all. Her work sometimes involved excruciatingly long hours for a couple of weeks or so and if a problem occurred in one of the families she was assigned to the last thing she wanted to worry about was watering plants.

She was concentrating so hard on descending gracefully, balanced as she was on her giddily high, needle-thin heels, that she didn't lift her head until she'd reached the safety of the tiled floor of the small entrance lobby.

'Wow.'

The deep male voice brought her head turning. Nick Morgan was leaning against the far wall, hands thrust in his pockets and black hair slicked back from his brow. He looked like something every red-blooded woman from the age of sixteen to sixty would love to find in their Christmas stocking. An exquisitely cut dinner jacket sat on shoulders broad enough to satisfy even the most demanding female, and the smile lighting up his blue eyes was electric.

Cory forgot to breathe as he walked towards her, only managing to mumble, 'Hello,' at the last moment.

'You look sensational.'

'Do I?' Oh, come on, you can do better than that. She wasn't totally without the ability of social repartee. She took hold of herself, adding, 'Thank you, you look pretty good yourself,' with a coolness she hoped he didn't know was completely feigned.

His gaze moved over her hair, eyes made up to look huge, and carefully painted lips, and there was a faint note of surprise in his voice when he said, 'You'll set tongues wagging tonight. They'll all want to know where I found you.'

He made it sound as though she was a stranded puppy he'd brought in from the cold. She forced a smile, saying lightly, 'I think it was the other way round, don't you? Or rather, it was Rufus who did the finding.' And then, because his comment really had caught her on the raw for some reason, she added sweetly, 'Perhaps it would be better if we didn't explain I had to pick you up from the floor.' She hadn't, not exactly, but if ever there was justification in stretching a point, Cory felt this was it.

He blinked, just once, but she knew she'd taken him aback. The smile dimmed a little for one thing. 'Quite.' He took her elbow. 'Shall we go?'

That had set the boundaries quite nicely; at least she hoped so. There was no way she was going to let this man patronise her, even if he did have the clout to take half of London to Templegate as his guests. Wealth did not equate to lordship, not in her book.

Once outside, even the heavily laden city fumes couldn't obliterate the beauty of a perfect June evening. The air was soft and warm, the buzz of the city lazy and evocative. Cory felt a little thrill of anticipation she wouldn't have thought herself capable of just minutes before.

Instead of the taxi she'd been expecting, she found herself led to a chauffeur-driven Mercedes. After seating her inside the vehicle, Nick Morgan joined her. 'Templegate, please, George,' he said easily, before settling himself more comfortably beside her. She could feel the imprint of a hard male thigh against her hip but didn't dare move. She wouldn't give him the satisfaction of thinking he bothered her in any way—if he was thinking along those lines, which he probably wasn't, of course.

Burningly aware of the way the slits in the dress revealed a tantalising amount of leg, Cory tried to think of something else. Nothing came to mind.

Too late she realised he'd said something and she'd missed it. 'I beg your pardon?' she said politely.

'I asked you if you'd been to Templegate before.'

It was slightly stiff as though he was offended about something. Cory suddenly wondered if he usually had to repeat himself when he was taking a woman out for the evening. She rather doubted it.

The surge of adrenalin this caused enabled her to say quite airily, 'No, I haven't as it happens although I've heard about the place, of course. One goes to see and be seen, I understand?'

'I wouldn't know about that.'

Oh, no. Right.

'The chef there is second to none, however.' He looked her full in the face as he spoke, forcing her to meet his gaze. The blue of his eyes was like the deepest ocean, something to drown in. 'And the guy in the cocktail bar, Luigi, is a master of his art. His drinks carry a sting in the tail that have made many a grown man wake up with the mother and father of a hangover the next morning.'

'Thanks for the warning,' she said tightly. He was too close. The confines of the luxurious car were too intimate. Her dress was too revealing. She turned her head to look out of the window.

There was a long pause when the air between them hinted at the delicious sensuality of his aftershave.

'Relax, Cory.'

It was the first time he had called her by her Christian name and it acted on her overwrought nerves like a cattle prod. 'Relax?' Her gaze shot to meet his again. 'I don't know what you mean. I'm perfectly relaxed.'

'Yeah?' He glanced meaningfully at her lap and for the first time she realised her hands were tight fists.

'Look, you won't be expected to do anything tonight,' he said quietly. 'Just enjoy yourself, okay? There are no hostess duties, if that's what's worrying you.'

She wasn't sure exactly what was worrying her but playing hostess was only part of it. She managed a little bounce of her head which could have passed for a nod. 'Your girl-friend,' she said awkwardly. 'She's not going to get the wrong idea about this?'

'Girlfriend?' Dark brows furrowed and then cleared. 'Oh, you mean Miranda? The model? No, she'll be fine. And, incidentally, she's a friend without the girl in front of it, if you get my meaning.'

She did. And she wasn't sure if that made her feel better or worse. Probably a bit of both. Which went with the general craziness of this whole evening.

'If we're supposed to be a couple—' again her eyes shot to his and he smiled innocently '—at least as far as my guests are concerned, I should know a bit about you, shouldn't I? Your work, hobbies, things like that.'

It sounded reasonable. It would have *been* reasonable if it was anyone but Nick Morgan. Which wasn't fair, Cory acknowledged silently. She didn't know him, not in the least, and he might be a very nice person under the arrogance and good looks and blatant wealth. William had been all those things too and she'd given him the benefit of the doubt, more fool her.

She smiled a brittle smile. 'I'm a social worker, working with disfunctional families on the whole. The hours are long, but when I'm not working I'm either eating, sleeping or preparing to do one or the other. Okay?'

He didn't say a word, merely continuing to observe her as the Mercedes purred through the evening traffic. Much to her annoyance, Cory found she was the one who looked away first.

She didn't know why she was loath to reveal anything about herself and her private life to this man, but the check was there, in her spirit. In truth she had lots of friends with whom she socialised and, although she had to do the odd intense stretch at work where she had no time to see anyone, these didn't occur all the time.

It was a good minute or two before he spoke again, and then his voice was bland. 'No time for fun then?'

'Not much, no.'

'Pity.'

'I don't think so.' He was really annoying her now, not by what he said but the tone in which he said it. But then it was her fault if he was pitying her. 'I love my work.'

'I enjoy mine but I still have a life outside it.'

'Like tonight?' she asked with a touch of sarcasm.

'Tonight, I admit, I'm combining work and pleasure.'

He didn't rise to her bait and Cory found herself feeling somewhat ashamed. She was being awful and she didn't understand why.

And then he slid shut the glass partition which gave them privacy from the driver, leaning towards her as he said softly, 'Are you always this prickly or is it me? Have I done something to offend you, Cory?'

She wished he wouldn't say her name like that, in that deep smoky way. Say something, she told herself. Anything to pass this off. She found she couldn't, her thought processes seemed to have faltered and died.

She cleared her throat, moistening her lips and then wishing she hadn't as the piercing gaze followed her tongue. 'I guess I'm just a little nervous,' she managed at last. 'Meeting your guests and so on.' She waved a vague hand. It wasn't the people though, just one person and he was sitting right beside her.

'You are more than a match for them.'

It was dry and she wasn't quite sure if he was complimenting her or not.

Her face must have revealed her thoughts because his searching gaze was replaced by a smile. 'You have a very open face,' he said, the smile lingering at the corners of his mouth. 'I would have thought that would've been a handicap in your line of work.'

She arched an eyebrow. 'I can be deadpan when I want

to be,' she assured him evenly. It was just that this capability didn't seem to work around Nick Morgan, although she wouldn't give him the satisfaction of admitting to it.

He settled back in the seat again and Cory breathed an inward sigh of relief as the space between them expanded.

'So the reason for your single status is down to work obsession?' he asked smoothly after a small pause.

She didn't answer this directly. 'I do not have a work obsession.'

Her voice had been clipped and again the corners of his mouth twitched. 'What else would you call it when a beautiful woman eats, sleeps and drinks her job?' he asked mildly.

'A career?' She couldn't remember when she'd last felt so mad with someone.

'A career doesn't exclude having friends—'

'I do have friends.'

'Or going on dates,' he continued as though unaware of her interruption.

'Look, Mr Morgan—'

'Nick.' The tone was amiable. 'Call me Nick or else my guests will think I've hired you for the evening.'

He had in a way. She put that fact to one side and concentrated on her main line of attack. 'I'm sorry but I really don't see that my lifestyle is any of your business,' she said hotly. 'You asked me to stand in for your girlfriend—'

'She's not my girlfriend. I thought we'd already ascertained that.'

'Whatever.' She put a wealth of disinterest into the word. 'Anyway, you asked me to stand in for her and I have. I don't think that that merits the third degree.'

'You think a little polite social intercourse qualifies as the third degree?' he asked with reproachful innocence.

Cory swallowed the words she wanted to say. They still

had the rest of the evening in front of them and some pretence at togetherness would be required, besides which she was blowed if she was going to rise to his bait. She breathed deeply, counted up to ten and smiled sweetly. 'One's definition of politeness can vary so much from person to person, don't you think, depending on background, upbringing, just how nice someone is?' she said with saccharine civility.

He knew exactly what she was really saying. Vivid blue eyes held defiant velvet-brown for a few moments and then, to her surprise, he threw back his head and laughed. 'You're a formidable lady, Miss Cory James. I have to admit I wondered how a slender young thing like you would be able to take on some big butch parent or other shouting about their rights. Now I know.'

Cory frowned. 'Do you usually stereotype people so harshly?' she said sharply. 'Most of my families are great people who are struggling to keep it together after a rotten start in life. They deserve every little bit of help and support they can get. It's people like you—' She stopped abruptly. The evening would certainly be over if she told him what she thought of people like him, and with her aunt paying a fortune for this dress and it having taken her hours to get ready she might just as well see the inside of Templegate!

It was very quiet in the car now. Then Nick said, 'You don't like me, do you.' It was a statement, not a question.

Cory chose not to say anything. The truth was apparent in her silence anyway.

'Why is that, I wonder?' he mused thoughtfully.

How long had he got? She nerved herself to glance at him. Bearing in mind he had been pretty reasonable about Rufus, as her aunt had pointed out, she prevaricated, 'I don't know you so how could I not like you?'

'If you'd put just the tiniest amount of warmth into that

I might have attempted to persuade myself you meant it,' he said drily. 'Is this state of hostilities going to continue all night because I think my guests might have severe indigestion at the end of it if so.'

She glared at him. 'I promised I'd accompany you and I wouldn't dream of being other than courteous to your guests.'

'I'm aware of that. I just thought they might find the evening something of a strain with you savaging their host at every opportunity.'

The underlying amusement in the deep voice made her want to hit him. Instead she called on all her self-control and said calmly, 'There's no question of that. I wouldn't do or say anything to embarrass them.'

'So I can count on you to give the impression we're the perfect couple?'

'Utterly,' she said with biting sarcasm.

'Love's young dream even?' he drawled lazily.

The quirk to his eyebrows and complete refusal to be affronted by her bad humour brought a reluctant smile to Cory's face. Impossible man!

'That's better.' He grinned at her and it did something powerful to the ruthlessly handsome face that made her heart race. 'Now, let me give you a quick who's who of who'll be there tonight, OK? They're a nice bunch on the whole but one or two are still a bit tender after the takeover. Understandable, but not conducive to good working relations. Hence this evening.'

Cory nodded. His tone had suddenly become very businesslike and that suited her down to the ground.

By the time the Mercedes drew up outside the chrome and glass building that was Templegate she'd absorbed most of the background information Nick had given her. She knew that five of the couples were married, including

the big chief, Martin Breedon, and that Martin and his wife
had recently been presented with their first grandchild.
'Good talking point,' Nick said cold-bloodedly. 'Folk are
always gaga over their grandchildren.' The remaining four
consisted of a couple who both worked at the company and
who were seeing each other, and a David Blackwell who
was bringing a date.

The chauffeur opened the car door but it was Nick who
assisted her out of the vehicle before saying, 'Bring the car
at three, OK, unless I ring before that,' whereupon he took
her arm and led her into the building.

Three o'clock? This was going to be one long night. And
then Cory's mind was washed clear of everything but her
immediate surroundings. The place was as expensively luxurious as she had expected and huge, but as Nick ushered
her into the cocktail bar, which was fairly buzzing, she
spotted at least three celebrities without even trying.

Closing her mouth, which she knew had fallen open, and
trying to appear as if she was completely au fait with the
milieu, Cory took the seat Nick had pulled out for her at a
table which overlooked the vast nightclub below. After
glancing at the cocktail menu, she tried to look for the least
alcoholic drink. She needed to keep all her wits about her
tonight and doubtless it would be one where the drinks
were flowing.

'If you're not sure, how about a champagne cocktail?'
Nick suggested quietly. 'I've ordered champagne for the
table.'

'Lovely.' She smiled brightly. Once he had walked
across to the massive circular bar which ran round three-
quarters of the room and behind which a number of waiters
were busy shaking mixers and juggling bottles with amazing dexterity, Cory studied the ingredients. Brandy, a couple of dashes of angostura bitters, dry champagne and a

white sugar cube. That didn't sound too lethal, certainly not compared to the Negroni, which was comprised of Campari, sweet vermouth and gin, or a Margarita, which looked pure dynamite. And she'd make the one last.

When Nick returned she took the champagne flute with a smile of thanks, lifting it in a salutation as she said, 'To a successful evening.'

'To a successful evening *and* my beautiful companion.'

She smiled again before taking a sip of the sparkling drink. It was delicious. She could well understand why the cocktail had been a favourite of stars of the silver screen in the forties; it epitomised the elegance and sophistication of that wonderful era beautifully.

'Well, this is very civilised.'

It could have been a pleasant social comment but she'd seen the wicked glitter in his eyes and knew he was making a point after her antagonism in the car. She decided to ignore it and take the words at face value. 'Isn't it,' she agreed lightly. 'And what a place this is. Like a film set.'

'The owner's always been a sucker for the sort of lavish decadence of the Fred Astaire, Ginger Rogers age. He set out to appeal only to the rich and famous, and he succeeded. There are more film stars, models and footballers here per square yard than anywhere else in the world.'

There was something, just the merest inflexion in the deep voice, which suggested he didn't altogether approve. Cory stared at him curiously. 'You're here,' she pointed out quietly, 'so you must enjoy all that too.'

'Must I?' It was laconic. And then as she continued to keep her eyes on him, he said, 'It's amusing to drop in now and again and undeniably useful for tonight's sort of occasion.'

'But you don't like it?' she persisted.

'I didn't say that.' The blue eyes surveyed her under

brows which suddenly had a moody tilt. 'It's just that I've found that wealth and fame don't always equate to good manners and acceptable behaviour. The desire to be a sensation and fêted and adored can be ugly when it becomes an obsession. Alex has made a fortune with Templegate and knows just how to keep the latest celebrity purring, whilst being able to take any tantrums and smooth ruffled plumage. I couldn't do that.'

She didn't doubt that for a minute. 'Alex?' she asked interestedly. 'Do you know the owner then?'

'We were at university together.' He paused, finishing his cocktail in one swallow before he said lazily, 'Care for another?'

'I'm fine.' She'd barely touched her own drink.

This time he raised a hand and immediately a waiter was at his side. After he'd given his order, Nick pointed out a well-known politician who had just entered the bar with a glamorous female on his arm who was easily young enough to be his daughter, if not his granddaughter, and then went on to mention other well-known faces he'd seen at Templegate. It wasn't until much later that Cory realised he'd turned the conversation away from himself most adeptly.

When the others arrived the atmosphere was a little tense at first, but Cory's misgivings about Nick's guests being standoffish were soon put to rest. With the exception of perhaps David Blackwell, the man who had brought along a date in the form of a tall willowy blonde who smiled a lot but who said little, she immediately felt at ease with them.

After cocktails, they were led to their table in the main section of the nightclub and Cory wasn't surprised it was in a prime position at the edge of the dance floor. The food was excellent, the floor show which entertained them while they ate equally so, and with the armour of the extravagant dress in place Cory felt as good as any of the other women in their designer evening wear.

The circular shape of the table prompted dialogue in which everyone could share, and she soon realised Nick had set himself out to be both charming and amusing. He was winning them all over, she mused, finishing the last of her pudding—a creamy orange charlotte—which had tasted heavenly, with real regret. Not that she would have eaten another morsel, she admitted to herself reluctantly, but each spoonful of the light, tangy dessert had been the stuff dreams were made of.

It was as the floor show ended and coffee arrived at the table that Cory noticed the look on David Blackwell's face. Everyone was laughing at something Nick had said, their amusement ably enhanced by the amount of very fine champagne which had been consumed, and David, who had just been to the men's cloakroom, was within a few feet of the table when she happened to glance his way. His bitter expression shocked her before he became aware of her gaze and immediately stitched a smile in place.

What was all that about? Cory asked herself, returning David's smile briefly before she turned back to Martin on her right as the older man spoke to her. What axe was David Blackwell grinding that made him so full of resentment towards Nick? And then she shrugged the thought away, telling herself it was none of her business and that it didn't matter anyway. After tonight she wouldn't see any of them again, including Nick, so any problem or disputes between Nick and David were unimportant to her. She was here to fulfil an obligation, that was all.

As though Nick had been aware of her thoughts, he now reached out a hand and covered one of hers where it was resting on her wineglass. 'Enjoying yourself?' he asked softly as her startled gaze met his. 'In spite of the reason you agreed to come?'

His flesh was warm and firm and a thousand little pinpricks shot out through her nerves at his touch. Ridiculous, she told herself. Ridiculous to react like this to a man you don't know and have no particular wish to know either. 'Yes, thank you,' she returned politely, slipping her hand away from under his on the pretext of reaching for her napkin to dab at the corners of her mouth.

'Good.' If he had noticed her withdrawal he didn't comment on it. 'Let's dance.'

'What?'

Before she'd had a chance to protest he had drawn her to her feet, his cool smile washing over the others as he said, 'The night's young, folks. Enjoy it.'

Before she knew where she was Cory found herself in his arms on the dance floor. There were only a few couples taking advantage of the slow, easy number the jazz combo were playing, but it wasn't that which had caused the sudden tension radiating through every nerve and sinew. His body was hard and strong, and held close to him like this his height was emphasised, making her feel fragile and feminine. It was a nice feeling. And she didn't want to have nice feelings around Nick Morgan. Neither did she want to acknowledge what the sensual scent of his aftershave was doing to her equilibrium.

She lifted her head, determined to say something to break the curiously intimate spell which seemed to have woven itself around them. His eyes were waiting for her, their blueness riveting, and causing the words to die in her throat as his body betrayed what her closeness was doing to him. 'You're one beautiful, sexy woman, Cory James,' he murmured huskily.

A tingle of excitement fluttered over her skin. It was a

warning and she knew it. William had said all the right things and before she'd known it she'd been in way over her head. She was never going to let that happen again. 'It's the dress,' she said, carefully and deliberately, forcing a flatness into her tone. 'Not me.'

He continued to look down at her and she prayed the trembling which had begun in her stomach wouldn't transfer itself to the rest of her body. The incredible width of his shoulders, the male squareness of his chin enhanced by the merest cleft and the ruggedness of the handsome face all proclaimed a virile masculinity which was overwhelming.

'No, it's not the dress,' he said softly, his eyes dark and intense. 'Although it's stunning.'

Stunning it might be but she regretted wearing it right now. No, no she didn't, she qualified in the next moment. She wanted to look sexy and beautiful to him. But then again it was the last thing she wanted. Which didn't make sense… Their gazes were still locked and she forced herself to break it, pulling back a little and glancing round the room as she said, 'It's a present, the dress. I didn't have anything remotely good enough for this place.' Suddenly the need to make him see they were poles apart was paramount.

'Who from?'

'What?' She glanced at him again.

'A present from whom?' he asked quietly, a look on his face now that Cory couldn't quite pin down.

'Oh, my Aunt Joan.' The music had changed and now a livelier number had drawn more people on to the dance floor. Cory noticed they were the only couple still entwined but when she tried to disentangle herself from his arms they merely tightened.

'Your Aunt Joan.' His face had cleared. 'Not an admirer then?'

'An admirer?' She stared at him, mingled surprise and outrage vying for first place. 'Of course not. As if I'd accept a present like this from a man.'

'It happens.' His voice was dry.

'Not with me it doesn't.' She glared at him.

'I'm very pleased to hear it.'

He was laughing at her! Oh, not openly, but she knew amusement was there in the tone of his voice and the way the firm, hard mouth was trying not to smile. 'You can let go of me for this dance,' she said frostily.

'Perhaps I don't want to let you go.'

'People are looking.'

'Let them look.' He bent his head and skimmed her mouth with his lips. 'There, that'll give them something to talk about,' he said evenly.

For one giddy instant the room swam. The caress had been too fleeting to be called a kiss but she'd felt the contact right down to her Covent Garden shod toes. She blinked. 'Don't do that, please,' she said as firmly as her breathing would allow. 'It's not in the agreement.'

'We didn't discuss the finer points, if I remember correctly.'

Cory ignored the little flame that had been ignited deep inside and frowned at him. 'Perhaps because I thought it wasn't necessary and that you were a gentleman.'

He grinned, completely unabashed. 'Big mistake,' he said cheerfully.

She ought to be furious at the arrogance but instead she found herself trying not to smile. But she couldn't let him suspect that. 'Shall I spell it out for you then?'

'Please do,' he said politely, laughter glinting in his eyes.

'I agreed to come here tonight because I'm in your debt about Rufus, but acting as your—'

'Girlfriend?' he put in helpfully.

'*Companion*,' she corrected firmly, 'only necessitates the most elementary bodily contact.'

He looked as though he was enjoying himself. 'Define elementary,' he said interestedly, his hand at her waist finding bare skin through one of the carefully positioned leaf transparencies and stroking it almost absent-mindedly.

Cory took a steadying breath. 'In this context elementary means straightforward, simple.' Her skin was melting. '*Rudimentary*,' she added desperately.

His head tilted as though he was considering what she'd just said. 'Sorry, can't agree to that.' His eyes danced over her hot face. 'Call it the interest on the debt if you like, but for this evening you're my consort and I'm not the kind of guy who is happy with…elementary bodily contact.'

In the same moment that the music finished Cory noticed David and the blonde at their elbow, the other man's close set eyes fastened avidly on their faces. It was enough to break the spell of Nick's closeness, and it enabled her to jerk away out of his arms. 'I'd like to sit down now, please.'

'Sure.' He took her hand, weaving his way through the couples on the dance floor and pulling out her chair for her when they reached their table.

Had David Blackwell been listening to their exchange? Cory tried to think exactly what had been said and what impression an eavesdropper might have formed as she sipped at her champagne, but it was difficult with the music and conversation all around. Making the excuse that she needed to visit the Ladies' cloakroom, she rose from the table, vitally aware of Nick's eyes on her as she left the room although she didn't glance his way.

Once in the relative quiet of the reception area she found the cloakroom—an elaborate affair of marble and mirrors—and sat down on one of the cream cushioned seats in the outer area to repair her lipstick. As her mind continued to dissect all that had been said on the dance floor she had to stop herself from groaning out loud. It might have sounded almost as if she was a hired escort of the most basic kind to anyone who didn't know the true facts.

She put the lipstick back in her purse, fiddling with her hair as her mind sped on. But then what she'd thought earlier still applied—she'd never see any of these people again so it didn't matter how they viewed her. She just didn't like someone like the Blackwell man getting the wrong idea, that was all. Admittedly she didn't know him but the guy gave her the creeps.

She straightened her back, her eyes narrowing as she stared at the reflection in the mirror. She wasn't going to worry about David Blackwell or anyone else for that matter. She'd fulfil her obligations tonight and make sure she went home alone in a taxi in view of Nick's earlier comments. She wasn't sure if he would be crass enough to try anything on when she'd made it clear how she felt, but she wouldn't give him the chance. The man was dangerous—she refused to qualify to herself that it was her response to him that was dangerous—and she didn't need any complications in her life at the moment.

When she stepped out of the cloakroom Cory had only taken a couple of steps when David caught hold of her wrist. He made her jump, having come up behind her, and her voice was sharp as she shook her hand free and said, 'Don't do that, please.'

'Sorry, sorry.' He was smiling but she'd noticed before that his smiles didn't reach his eyes. 'I just wanted a word with you, that's all.'

'Couldn't it have waited until we're at the table?'

'In private.' His voice was low. 'I wanted to speak to you in private, Cory.'

She didn't like the way he spoke her name in that slightly conspiratorial tone and her voice reflected this when she said, 'I don't know you. How could we have anything to discuss privately?'

'Look, I'll come clean.'

He was too close and the amount of aftershave he was wearing was making her feel nauseous. It had a sickly sweet scent with a tang of something else beneath it, much like the man himself, she suspected.

'I couldn't help overhearing what you and Nick were saying on the dance floor and I take it you aren't his actual girlfriend?'

Cory stared into the weasely face. Was this a come-on, because if it was he'd get more than he'd bargained for.

When she neither confirmed nor denied this, he went on, 'The thing is, I suppose you know he's just taken over the firm, lock, stock and barrel? A lot of people were upset at first but they've all gone quiet, pay-offs I suppose,' he added bitterly.

Where was this going? 'That's nothing to do with me.'

'I know that but—' He paused. 'Look, it was clear from what he said that he fancies you and that you aren't interested. Most women fall in adoration at his feet.' Again hot resentment came through loud and strong. 'That being the case, I'd make it worth your while if you could find out a couple of things for me.'

'What?' She stared at him in absolute amazement.

'If you just jollied him along I'm sure he'd talk to you. You know, pillow talk. You could ask him about the takeover and how people were, whether he paid on the quiet to get Martin's co-operation, things like that. I reckon I'm the only one who hasn't had a backhander and it's not fair.'

He wanted a backhander? She'd give him one right round his nasty little face if he said another word. And *pillow* talk? How dared he? 'If you want to know anything about Mr Morgan's dealings with the rest of your associates I suggest you ask him yourself,' Cory said icily. 'OK?'

His eyes narrowed at her tone but then a wheedling note came into his voice. 'That'd be no good, facing him head on like that. It's the ladies who are his weakness. You could get more out of him with just being friendly than I could in a month of Sundays. He wouldn't suspect anything if that's what's worrying you. He's used to women throwing themselves at him all the time.'

'Really?' If she'd been anywhere else but her present surroundings, Cory would have socked him on the jaw. 'And I wonder why that is? Could it be that he is a real man rather than a snivelling little excuse for one? You picked the wrong woman to ask to do your dirty work, Mr Blackwell, and the minute I go back into that room Mr Morgan will be told of your proposition, all right?'

'That won't be necessary.'

The deep, cold voice behind them made them both jump a mile, and Cory found herself tottering on the exorbitantly high heels for a breathtaking moment. Like David, she'd spun round with more haste than care. Righting herself, she saw a different Nick from the one she'd known all evening. This one was frightening.

'Nick.' David's voice was sickeningly obsequious. 'This isn't what you think.'

'Save it.' The blue eyes could have been cut from granite. 'This isn't the time or the place. My office on Monday morning. Eight o'clock sharp.'

'But let me explain—'

'There's no time, you're leaving.' Nick raised his hand and as though by magic one of the staff was at his elbow. 'Would you be so good as to tell Miss Miller on table twelve that Mr Blackwell is waiting out here for her, please?'

As the man hurried away David tried again, and Cory felt like telling him it was no use.

Nick cut into David's servile excuses after the first sentence. 'We might just keep this civilised if you disappear right now,' he said grimly, 'but don't push your luck, David. Not tonight. Ah, Fiona...' As the blonde appeared with a puzzled expression on her pretty face, Nick waved his hand at David, saying, 'I'm afraid David is indisposed but I'm sure he'll see you safely home. Goodnight.'

As Nick took Cory's arm and walked her away, he murmured, 'Do you want a few minutes to compose yourself before we join the others?'

Did birds fly? Her head was spinning and she didn't know if she was on foot or horseback. She nodded, and the next minute she found herself ensconced in the cocktail bar, which was now almost completely deserted. Sinking down on to a seat, she said faintly, 'What will you do to him?'

'Don't worry about David Blackwell; his type always come up smelling of roses.' As the waiter came over, Nick said to her, 'Another cocktail?'

'Is it possible to have a coffee instead?' She felt a little tipsy as it was.

'Make that two, please.'

The waiter looked as though he was going to protest for a moment, but after a glance at Nick's face he said quickly, 'Two coffees it is, sir,' and disappeared.

'For the record, there have been no hand-outs.' Nick looked her straight in the eye. 'It's true Martin didn't want to relinquish the reins but we reached a compromise where we're both happy. Unfortunately the guy's too soft for his own good and has carried a lot of dead wood for years—like David Blackwell—so there will be changes to be made. I'm sure David's got wind of that and is feeling threatened.'

'I think he feels a lot more threatened now.'

'With good cause.' And then so suddenly that it made Cory catch her breath, his face changed, his voice warm and throaty as he said, 'Thanks for being on my side out there.'

She didn't know what to say. She shrugged uncomfortably. If he'd heard the bit about the hand-outs he'd been there longer than she would have liked.

Like before, he seemed to know what she was thinking, his voice now holding a thread of amusement when he murmured, 'I especially liked the bit about me being a real man.'

'A gentleman wouldn't mention he'd heard that,' she said, knowing she'd gone a bright crimson.

'I thought we'd already ascertained that I'm not a gentleman.' His smile lit the flame inside again and this time it burnt stronger.

Cory was very glad when the coffee arrived a moment later.

CHAPTER THREE

CONTRARY to what she had expected after the unpleasant incident with David Blackwell, Cory found she thoroughly enjoyed the rest of the evening.

When they returned to the table Nick said briefly that David was feeling unwell and had had to leave early. Which was true in a way. The other man had certainly looked green about the gills when they'd left him.

No one seemed particularly concerned or interested that David and Fiona were no longer with them; in fact with the young man's departure the whole group seemed more relaxed and natural, in Cory's opinion. She wondered just how much David had been whispering in people's ears about Nick. A little yeast could very quickly work through a batch of dough, and David had seemed resentful of Nick as a person as well as an employer, as the remarks about Nick being popular with the ladies had shown.

Everyone stayed right to the end of the evening at three o'clock, whereupon they all declared they'd had a night to remember. Cory could agree with this as a good part of it had been spent in Nick's arms on the dance floor.

She'd put the idea of going home in a taxi to one side. Somehow the episode with David had taken her and Nick beyond such a thing. Now, as everyone said goodnight amid hugs and handshakes, the possibility that Nick might expect more than a goodnight peck was at the forefront of her mind. It excited her as much as it scared her. She couldn't get involved with Nick—every nerve and bone in her body was telling her so. He was way, way out of her league in every respect.

He'd probably not want to see her again anyway. Men the whole world over seemed capable of nipping in and out of bed with this woman or that without it really meaning a thing to them and, from what David had said, Nick was never short of female company.

But she was jumping the gun here. He hadn't suggested bed. He hadn't suggested anything.

Slow down, she warned herself silently. Stop panicking. You are a grown woman of twenty-five who is more than capable of taking care of herself in every way, not a fifteen-year-old schoolgirl.

They waited until all of Nick's guests were safely on their way home in the fleet of taxis he'd ordered, and then he led her over to the Mercedes, which was parked across the road. 'Care to come back to my place for a nightcap?' he asked softly as he opened the car door for her.

'No.' It was too quick and now she moderated her refusal with a smile as she said, 'I'm exhausted; it's been a long day.'

He nodded, joining her in the car and sliding the glass panel which separated them from the driver to one side. 'Back to Miss James's place please, George,' he said quietly before closing it shut again and then pulling a blind down so they were now quite private.

Cory went into overdrive. More flustered than she'd ever been in her life, she searched for something, anything, to distract him. Then she found herself saying, 'I wondered if we'd see your friend, Alex, tonight but he didn't appear.'

'He's in the States.'

'Really?' She was burningly aware of a hard male thigh against hers. 'On holiday or business?'

'Holiday.'

'In what state?' she gabbled. 'America's such a huge country, isn't it, and so fascinating. I think—'

She never did tell him what she thought because he kissed her. Really kissed her. And it was everything she'd imagined it might be. Hot, stunningly sweet and altogether mind-blowing.

She could tell he was devastatingly experienced, a man who would know a woman's weakness and just how to use it for his own advantage in the seduction stakes. The warning in her mind was there but it didn't mean a thing while his mouth was working its magic and his arms were pressing her close to his hardness.

Almost leisurely, he explored her mouth until her heart thudded wildly against the steady beat of his and she was kissing him back in total surrender.

This was crazy, insane. She knew that, knew she had to call a halt before things got out of hand, but it was impossible with her blood singing through her veins and molten lava in the pit of her stomach. His hands were clever, stroking her arms and the smooth roundness of her shoulders until her skin was on fire with his caresses.

She gave herself over totally to the kiss, knowing the danger of letting herself become vulnerable to this man but unable to help herself. He kissed so well; she had never been kissed like this in all her life. She'd found most men used a kiss as a preliminary to other things but Nick seemed in no hurry to progress, seemingly enjoying her mouth as much as she was relishing his.

His hands moved up to her hair and within a moment it was falling down about her shoulders, silky soft and smelling of apple blossom shampoo. His fingers tangled themselves in the rich strands, using them to draw her head backwards to allow him greater access to the sensitive skin of her throat.

Cory moaned softly, her hands sliding over the powerful male chest muscles flexing beneath his shirt. The faint scent of aftershave she'd noticed earlier was teasing her nostrils again, its essence wild and dangerous, feeding her desire with its elusive aroma.

She heard him whisper her name as his mouth came back to hers, his voice husky. She knew what he wanted because she wanted it too, and it didn't seem to matter where they were or what the rest of the world was doing.

The thought was enough to bring her abruptly to her senses. This was a William Patterson situation all over again. *He'd* had charisma and that extra something which was undefinable but which made a woman go weak at the knees. *He* had pursued her, using his wealth and magnetism to dazzling effect until she hadn't known if black was white. She'd been wary at first. Why would a man like William, fifteen years older than her, rich, successful, be bothering with a little nobody fresh out of university? She'd been right to be wary. She should have gone on being wary…

She had stopped kissing Nick back and unconsciously stiffened as the memories had flooded in, and now she became aware that he had picked up on her withdrawal as he drew away. 'What's wrong?' he asked very quietly, but without the annoyance or irritation she'd half-expected.

'I…I don't do this, not on the first date.' Although it wasn't a date, as she'd reminded him this evening. Which made everything a hundred times worse.

'You don't kiss?'

His voice was still without expression and, because she could only catch glimpses of his face now and again by the light of passing streetlamps, she had no idea if he was angry or not. She didn't know how to answer him. How could she say that what they'd just shared had been more than a kiss, at least to her? That would give all the wrong signals. And to admit she had presumed it was the prelude to something more would be even worse.

Cory swallowed. 'Not like this, no.'

'Like this?'

'In…in the back of a car.' She swallowed again. 'A goodnight kiss on the doorstep is one thing, but this is more…'

'Intimate?' he finished for her.

'Yes.'

'Nice, though.' There was warmth in his voice now and she was glad of the darkness to hide her burning cheeks. There was a pause and then he said, 'OK, no more kissing until I deposit you on your doorstep.' Before she could resist, his arm had gone round her and he drew her into his side, holding her against him, pushing her head down on to his shoulder. 'Relax,' he said softly. 'Shut your eyes and think of that doorstep.'

'Nick—'

'No more talking, not unless you want me to remember I'm not a gentleman.'

Relax he'd said, with every nerve she possessed twanging and her heart thumping fit to burst at his closeness.

It seemed a long, long time until the Mercedes purred to a halt outside the flat. Cory knew exactly how a jelly must feel.

'Your doorstep awaits, Ma'am.' The deep voice was smoky with amusement.

From some unexpected reserve of self-preservation, Cory managed to feign sleepiness as she raised her head from the pillow of his shoulder. 'Are we here?' she mumbled, pretending to yawn. 'I must have been dozing.'

He didn't challenge her on the lie, but there was a distinctly quizzical slant to his mouth as he exited the car and then helped her out.

The night air wasn't cold—in fact there was a humid balminess to the shadowed street which suggested another hot June day in store—but Cory shivered as his big hand closed over her fingers. When she was standing on the pavement she tried to gently disentangle herself from his hold, but Nick was having none of it.

Instead he pulled her to the front door of the house. 'Come on,' he said coolly. 'In we go.'

'There's no need for you to come up,' she protested quickly. 'Thank you for a lovely evening and—'

'I'm seeing you to your front door.' It was spoken in a tone which brooked no argument. 'I'd never forgive myself if a mad axeman was lying in wait,' he added with every appearance of seriousness.

She didn't trust the solemnity any more than she trusted him. 'I hardly think that's likely.'

'No? You want to look at the news and read the papers more often. Rape, pillage, mayhem and destruction are all part of the world we live in,' he said cheerfully. 'Do you want me to open the door?'

'I'm quite capable, thank you.' Having said that the keys had got themselves jammed in the lining of the purse somehow, and it took a few moments to yank them free under his amused gaze.

Once inside the hall, Cory whispered, 'You'll have to be very quiet. The people on this floor have a dog that hears the slightest thing and then barks enough to wake the dead.'

'Wonderful,' Nick murmured sarcastically.

'It is, actually. It makes everyone feel very safe.'

'Haven't they heard of burglar alarms?'

A low growl from across the hall persuaded Cory to give up the argument. She slipped off her sandals preparatory to climbing the stairs and, as she straightened, he whispered, 'You've just lost about five inches. What have you been walking on all night, stilts?'

She couldn't help giggling. 'You wait till you see my glass eye and wooden leg.'

'I can't wait.'

As they reached the first landing where her flat was all amusement left Cory however. Was he expecting to be asked in for a nightcap? Was he expecting to be asked in for something else? Or both? But she'd made it plain how she felt in the car—she hoped. But if he kissed her again…

'Thank you for a lovely evening,' she began.

'You've already done that bit.' He had to bend further to kiss her this time now she was minus the sandals, and it was still more satisfying than the most expensive chocolate. All the feelings he'd aroused in the car were there, and her arms were just beginning to snake up to his shoulders when she was free. 'Goodnight, Cory,' he said blandly.

Goodnight? She stared at him, totally taken aback, before she pulled herself together. 'Goodnight,' she said quickly. 'And I meant what I said, by the way. It was a lovely evening.'

He smiled, his eyes glittering in the dim light on the landing. 'I thought so.' His hand reached out and stroked the silky skin at the side of her face below her ear.

Cory had never realised there were so many nerve-endings in one place. Should she ask him in and blow the consequences? The force of the temptation was so strong it was enough to kill it. Besides, he had already turned and walked to the head of the stairs.

'Sleep well,' he said lazily.

He wasn't going to ask to see her again. Well, she'd expected pretty much that, hadn't she? And if he had, she'd determined she'd say no anyway.

'Fancy lunch tomorrow?'

Her heart did an Olympic leap and then raced for gold. The moment of truth. *Remember William.* She didn't want to remember William, she wanted to say yes. Which was why it had to be no. 'Lunch?' she repeated weakly.

'You know, that meal in between breakfast and dinner?'

It was easier when he was being sarcastic. 'I don't think so, thank you.'

'Why not?' He rested his arms on the banister, his face full of sharply defined planes and angles in the shadows.

'Because—' She hesitated. Should she lie and say she had a prior engagement? But he'd only suggest another time. 'Because I'm not dating at the moment.'

'The work thing.' He shook his head. 'Not a good enough reason when your dog damn near broke my back.'

'I've made recompense for that,' she said indignantly. 'And Rufus isn't my dog anyway.'

'You were in charge of him.' He grinned. 'Do you want to see my bruises?'

'Not particularly.' He was doing the charm bit again and it was lethal. Good job William had made her immune to such ploys.

'There are women who'd die for the privilege.'

'I don't doubt it.' She was determined not to smile.

'I'll be back at midday. There's a great little pub I know where the roast beef melts in the mouth and the Yorkshire puddings are more than puffs of air.'

'I've told you, I'm not dating,' she said severely.

'And I've told you, this isn't a date but more paying off your debt. I don't like to eat Sunday lunch alone.' He straightened. 'OK?' he threw over his shoulder as he began to walk down the stairs.

Not OK. Definitely not OK, but it was like saying no to a brick wall. She followed him to the top of the stairs, looking down at his back as she hissed, 'Nick, I'm not having Sunday lunch with you.'

'Twelve sharp.' He turned just long enough for her to see the flash of his white teeth in the darkness. 'And I'm not backing off, Cory, so accept with good grace.'

'Nick!'

He was in the hall now and his voice was low and reproachful when he murmured, 'Quiet, remember the dog.'

She muttered something very rude about the dog just as the front door closed behind him.

In spite of the late hour, after Cory had showered and removed her make-up she found she was wide awake. The events of the evening were spinning through her head like a fast moving film and sleep was a million miles away. She tossed and turned for an hour or more before getting out of bed and padding through to the kitchen.

A mug of hot milk and half a packet of chocolate digestive biscuits later, she tried to get a handle on the way her life had been turned upside down in less than twenty-four hours.

The man was a human bulldozer, she told herself irritably. It would serve him right if she was out tomorrow when he called.

But she wouldn't be.

She sighed. This was madness. Getting involved with a man like Nick Morgan, even briefly, was asking for trouble. Unbidden, thoughts of William intruded and for once she was too muddled and over-tired to stop them.

When she had met him she had left university six months earlier and had been training for her present job. She and her colleagues had treated themselves to a Christmas meal at an expensive restaurant and it had been there she'd bumped into him—quite literally. The heel of one of her shoes had suddenly snapped and she'd fallen against him.

She reached for another biscuit, needing the sweetness to combat the acidity of the memories.

She had known from the beginning that William was wrong for her, that he was the type of man who would never be happy settling down with just one woman. But he had pursued her, probably because she was a challenge. Normally women fell into his lap like ripe plums and it had been something of a novelty for him to be the hunter for once. She had known that, in her head, but in spite of that she had found herself falling for him. Some little grain of sense, of sanity—call it what you would—had prevailed, however, and in spite of all his efforts he hadn't got her into his bed.

Then he had asked her to marry him.

The packet of biscuits had almost gone now. Feeling mad at herself for the self-indulgence, Cory stuffed the remainder back in the biscuit barrel and turned off the kitchen light, padding back to her bedroom and climbing into bed.

She had been over the moon at William's proposal. It had meant he wanted her, *really* wanted her and not just as a sexual conquest. For the first time in her life she had felt loved, the hang-ups from her lonely childhood and teens fading into the distance.

He'd suggested a weekend in Paris to celebrate the engagement, declaring he knew the most perfect little jeweller's shop there where she could choose her ring. She'd said yes—who wouldn't? Of course she'd known that 'celebrating' would probably mean more than the limited love-making she'd allowed so far, but they were going to be married...

Why she had called unannounced at the advertising agency William owned the night before they were due to leave for Paris, she didn't really know. She had been visiting a problem family in Soho, and rather than go straight home she'd decided to stroll the mile or so to the agency in Mayfair. With hindsight it had been the worst—and the best—thing she could have done.

Nearly everyone had left by the time she got there, but after assuring William's secretary—whom she'd met at the door—that she'd surprise him, she had made her way to his office on the top floor of the building. And she'd surprised him all right, as well as the partially clothed blonde he had been writhing with on the couch.

The scene which had followed had been ugly. He'd accused her of being frigid, an emotional cripple and plenty more besides in an effort to justify himself. She had walked out and had never seen him again from that day to this. A very messy end to an affair which never should have started in the first place.

Cory sighed, turning over in bed and hammering at her pillow, which felt as if it was packed with rocks. She had to get some sleep; she'd look like a wet rag in the morning. She began the technique she'd perfected in the months after William's betrayal, relaxing all her muscles, one by one, from the bottom of her feet to the top of her head.

Half an hour later she was as wide awake as ever, but this time it was Nick Morgan who was featuring on the screen in her mind.

She must have drifted off at some point after it became light, because when the alarm woke her at nine o'clock she was in the middle of a particularly erotic dream which made her blush to think about it.

How could she imagine such antics with a man she'd only met the day before? she asked herself in the shower. She could still feel the electricity racing through her veins which she'd experienced in the dream when Nick had touched and tasted her, and the heat in her body was nothing to do with the warm water cascading down on her. Crazy. She turned the dial to cold. It didn't help much.

He was early—fifteen minutes early—but as Cory had spent the last two hours agonising over what to wear, she was ready. Her bedroom looked like a bomb had hit it and almost every single item of clothing she possessed was on the bed or floor, but Nick wasn't going to go in that particular room so it didn't matter. She closed the door firmly. In fact she'd made up her mind he wasn't going to set foot in the flat let alone her bedroom. This lunch was going to be the end of the road. Just the state she'd got in over what to wear had convinced her of that.

After William she hadn't had a date for some time, but when she'd felt ready to go into the arena again she had made sure any hopeful suitors understood pretty quickly that what she had to offer was limited. Fun, friendship, the odd kiss and cuddle but nothing heavy. She had no intention of letting a man into her life, her mind or her body. She needed to be in control of any relationship from the beginning, and she ended things immediately if any man couldn't keep to the rules of engagement.

She didn't want to suffer pain again. As she pressed the intercom and told him she would be straight down, Cory's mouth was tight. Her parents had been unable to love her as parents normally did and William had just reaffirmed that there must be something lacking in her. Something which caused people not to want her like she wanted them. So she'd concentrate on her work, on making a difference in an area where she *was* needed. And that would suffice. It would, because it had to.

She hadn't opened the front door of the building for him this time, so when she stepped out into the hot June day

Nick was leaning against a snazzy little black sports car parked across the road. He looked…disturbing. His pale blue shirt was tucked into the flat waistband of his trousers and was unbuttoned just enough at the neck to show the beginning of the soft black hair on his chest.

Narrow-waisted and lean-hipped, he had a flagrant masculinity that was impossible to ignore. It was intimidating, and that made her annoyed because she didn't want to feel intimidated. It put her at a disadvantage even though he couldn't know how she felt.

'Hi.' He walked towards her, his thickly lashed blue eyes appreciative as they took in the pale rose jeans and bubble gum pink flounced strapless top she was wearing. She had left her hair loose today, wearing only a touch of mascara and lip gloss, the wide silver hoops in her ears completing the picture of casual elegance for a hot summer's day. She had been determined not to dress up too much and by the same token wore the minimum of make-up; she hadn't wanted him to think she was making an effort—even if it had taken over two hours to decide on her look.

'Hello.' She knew her cheeks matched her top but she couldn't do a thing about it.

'I'm glad you decided to come,' he said softly.

Decided to come? She'd been railroaded by an expert and he knew it. She sucked in a shaky breath but her voice was surprisingly firm when she said, 'The way I remember it, I had little choice?'

'Ouch.' He pretended to wince. 'You were supposed to say, preferably with a sweet smile, that you were glad I'd asked you, that you've been looking forward to it, something like that.'

'Really?' She provided the sweet smile. 'But I don't lie very well.'

He grinned at her, apparently totally unabashed. 'Then

I'll just have to work hard today to make sure you're looking forward to our next date, won't I?'

No way, no how. If ever she'd needed proof she'd inadvertently caught a tiger by the tail, it was in that grin. The word charm had obviously been invented with Nick Morgan in mind. She tried very hard to ignore her racing heart. 'Surely your model—Miranda, isn't it?—is back from the States soon?'

They had just reached the car and he brought her round to face him with both hands on her shoulders. He gave her a hard look. 'One, Miranda isn't *my* anything. Two, I've no idea when she returns because she's not obliged to report her whereabouts to me. Three...' His frown changed to a quizzical ruffle. 'Three, have you any idea what the feel of your bare shoulders is doing to me?'

Possibly. His shirt was thin and the dark shadow beneath it suggested his powerful chest was thickly covered with hair.

Cory took the coward's way out. 'No Mercedes today?' she said brightly, hoping he wouldn't notice the slight croakiness to her voice as she turned and pretended an interest in the car. 'Is this yours too?'

'Weekend runabout.' He opened the passenger door. 'Purely to impress my legion of women, of course.'

She decided to ignore the sarcasm. After sliding into the car, which gave the sensation that one was sitting at a level with the road, she straightened her back and folded her hands in her lap so she wouldn't make the mistake of bunching them again and betraying her tenseness as she'd done the night before.

When Nick joined her, it took all of Cory's control to maintain the pose. The close confines within the car was the ultimate in travelling intimacy and wildly seductive.

As he started the engine she glanced at him. 'Where are we going?' she asked with careful steadiness.

'Surprise.'

'I don't like surprises.'

'Tough.' The blue eyes did a laser sweep of her face. 'But don't worry, I'm not into spiriting women away and forcing my wicked will on them. Not on a Sunday lunchtime anyway,' he added lazily.

'I never thought you were.' She hoped the haughty note had come through in her voice.

'No?' He swung the streamlined panther of a car smoothly into the Sunday traffic, his gaze on the road. 'You could have fooled me. I'm getting the distinct impression you view me as the original Don Juan.'

'Not at all,' she said stiffly, refusing to dwell on how large and capable his hands looked on the leather-clad steering wheel, or how those same hands had caressed her last night in the back of the Mercedes.

'Good.' It was casual, as though he didn't care much one way or the other, and as she glanced at him again she saw a small smile was playing about the firm mouth. 'So, tell me a bit about yourself,' he went on. 'I gather you have an aunt living around here with a broken leg. Any more family? And what about siblings to take turns with Rufus the terrible?'

Cory's heart plummeted. She didn't want to talk about herself, not to him. She had the feeling that the less Nick knew about her, the better. Still, she could hardly refuse to tell him the basics. 'My parents died some years ago,' she said flatly, 'and I don't have any brothers or sisters. My Aunt Joan is my closest relative.'

'And you get on well with her?'

'Oh, yes.' She was unaware of the sudden warmth in her voice but the big man at the side of her noted it. 'She's always been more than an aunt to me. My parents…well, they were busy people. They didn't have a lot of time…' Her voice trailed away as she became aware she was in danger of revealing too much.

'A peaceful childhood then? With lots of friends to make up for the lack of brothers and sisters?' he asked casually.

Lots of friends? She had never been allowed to bring friends home or invite anyone round for tea, neither had she been permitted to go to other children's houses when they had invited her. It had been too much trouble for her parents, interfering with their plans. The string of au pairs her parents had had all through her childhood had been instructed to make sure that, once she had been given her tea, she was despatched up to her room to do her homework. After that she had been allowed to read or watch TV, but never encouraged downstairs except to say goodnight. Her room had been spacious with its own *en suite* bathroom, and the TV and all her things had been of the best, but it had still felt like a prison.

Cory's stomach clenched. She looked away through the side window so he had no chance of seeing her face if he glanced at her, the silky curtain of her hair swinging forward. 'It was quite peaceful at home,' she agreed evenly.

If he noticed that she had only answered half his question he didn't comment on it. 'Any pets?'

In her mother's immaculate surroundings? 'No, no pets,' she said quietly. 'What about you? Do you have family living near?'

'Depends whether you think Barnstaple is near. I was brought up there and my mother still lives there although my father died five years ago.'

There was a note in his voice which prompted her to say, 'I'm sorry. Were you close?'

'Very. He was a great guy. But my mother has my two

sisters and their families to keep her busy; they both live within walking distance from the old house. I have a property in the area too, but due to the business I'm away more than I'm at home. Hence the flat in London.'

'So you had a happy childhood?' she asked curiously, drawn by the affection in his deep voice as he'd spoken about his family.

'The best.' They had just drawn up at some traffic lights and again the blue gaze raked her face. 'Hence the nicely rounded, well-adjusted individual you see in front of you,' he said quietly.

The lights changed in the next instant but, as the car purred on, the content of his last words stayed with Cory. Had he been hinting that she wasn't those things or was she being over-sensitive here? she asked herself silently, her mouth unconsciously tightening. If it was the former then he'd got a right cheek because she was fine, just fine. But it could be the latter...

She risked another sideways glance through her eye-lashes. It probably wasn't the moment to notice the way his dark hair curled ever so slightly into the base of his neck. It wasn't short and it wasn't long but it suited him perfectly. She wondered how it would feel if she sifted her fingers through the soft strands. And then she caught the errant thought quickly and looked straight ahead before he caught her observing him.

She was going loopy here. What on earth was she doing fantasising about this man? In fact, how come she was with him in the first place? She wanted her head examined!

By the time they reached the pub, which was close to Hampstead Heath, Cory just wanted out of the car. She couldn't ever remember being so aware of every little movement or action by another human being. Nick, on the other hand, appeared perfectly relaxed and at ease, chatting about this and that and keeping the conversation strictly impersonal now.

Once inside the pub, which was all brass and copper and leaded windows, he led her straight through and out into the small, flower-bedecked garden at the rear. 'This is our table.' He pointed to a table for two set next to a lattice of climbing roses which were scenting the air with their rich sweetness.

'How do you know?' The pub had been packed inside and out here the few tables there were were full.

Nick reached out and removed a reserved sign from the table. 'Trust me,' he said, smiling. 'I know the owner.'

'Not another university friend?'

'Boyhood friend this time. John and I grew up together.'

'And he always keeps this table for you?'

'If I ring up and request it, yes. Which I did first thing this morning.' He pulled out a sun-warmed seat and she sank down, the perfume of the flowers and the caress of the sun on her skin blissful.

'They do a great Brunello here,' Nick said, still standing. 'Do you like red wine?'

'Love it.'

'I'll get a bottle. I shall limit myself to one glass as I'm driving but I guarantee once you taste it, you'll be unable to resist another. Shall I order two roast dinners while I'm at it?'

Cory nodded. This was nice, too nice.

So was the wine when it came. The intense chocolate and nutty aroma was a ripe explosion of taste in the mouth, and she closed her eyes and just breathed in the aroma made all the more potent by the hot air. 'This is gorgeous,' she murmured, taking another long sip.

'Don't tell me I've found the way to your heart?' Nick

had sat down opposite her, his eyes slightly closed against the sun and his long legs stretched out in front of him.

Forget about the roast dinner, Cory thought wryly. He looked good enough to eat. She raised an eyebrow. 'With one glass of wine?' she said severely. 'I think not.'

'The bottle's there, feel free.'

She smiled. 'I've always believed in moderation in all things.'

'All things?' The blue eyes were wicked.

'*All* things,' she insisted firmly, refusing to acknowledge the innuendo.

'Then it's as I thought,' Nick said with obvious complacency. 'Your education in certain areas has been sadly neglected and I look upon it as my duty to set things right. What you need to do from this point, Cory, is to look upon me as your teacher and guide into the ways of the flesh. OK?' And he took a long, satisfying drink of wine.

She laughed. Well, there was nothing else she could do really, because she couldn't take him seriously. In spite of the bolt of lightning that had shot through her.

'I'm more than up to the task,' he assured her softly, putting down the glass and taking one of her hands in his. He turned her fingers over so that the soft, vulnerable underside of her wrist was exposed, stroking it with first one finger and then—shockingly—as he raised her hand to his mouth, his warm lips.

'Don't!' She snatched her hand away, almost knocking the wine over. 'Don't do that.'

'Why not?' He sat back in his chair, his eyes on hers. 'It's nothing.' His smile was lazy.

It *was* nothing and yet it suggested everything—all the forbidden delights of her dream were in those warm, knowing lips. She knew exactly what he was trying to do and she was determined not to acknowledge her own desire and need. She shrugged. 'I don't play those sort of games,' she said shortly.

There wasn't even a hint of a smile on his lips when he said, 'Who's playing games?'

CHAPTER FOUR

CORY could have kissed the little barmaid who arrived at the table with their food just after Nick had spoken. In the ensuing activity the moment for her to respond to him came and went, and she made sure she tucked into her meal without further ado. The Sunday roast with all the trimmings was delicious, as was the hazelnut and cherry pie which followed, all washed down with another large glass of wine by Cory and sparkling mineral water for Nick.

Nick's friend brought their coffee, pulling up a chair from a table which had been vacated when Nick invited him to join them for a glass of wine. 'Here.' Nick poured the last of the wine into his empty glass and passed it to John. 'Cory insists she's had enough.'

'Potent stuff, isn't it?' John was a slight blond man and he grinned at Cory as he spoke. 'My favourite ever since Nick introduced me to it years ago. Bit expensive for the pub trade but I always make sure a bottle's in for when this guy turns up.' He punched Nick lightly on the shoulder. 'I can only stay a minute or two, though. Lucinda—the wife,' he added in an aside to Cory, 'will be on the warpath if she catches me slacking.'

'Are you man or mouse?' Nick put in.

'Where Lucinda's concerned? Definitely rodent.'

He was only halfway through the glass and in the middle of relating an incident from their childhood—about the time when he and Nick had been caught scrumping from a farmer's orchard—when the said Lucinda appeared. Big, buxom and definitely Italian, she bustled over to their table,

66

throwing her arms round Nick and then scolding him for staying away for too long, before she clipped her husband round the ear. 'You creep out here without telling me and then you drink the last of Nick's wine,' she remonstrated in a heavy accent. 'You are the impossible man. You see what I have to put up with?' she appealed to Nick. 'And who is your beautiful lady?' she added, turning a beaming smile on a bemused Cory.

'Cory James meet Lucinda Robinson,' Nick said, laughter in his voice. 'And her bark's worse than her bite.'

'Says who?' said John, rubbing his ear. 'She used to do that when she was a little thing the size of Cory but I could keep her in her place then. She packs a fair wallop now.'

'Oh, you.' Lucinda planted a smacking kiss on John's lips, pinching his bottom as she added, 'I keep you warm at night though, yes?'

'That you do, wench.' John smiled at his wife and for a moment the look the two exchanged brought a lump to Cory's throat. This was love, true love. It was shining out of their faces. For a second she envied the other woman from the bottom of her heart.

After a few more minutes, during which time Lucinda had extracted a promise from Nick that he would attend her thirty-fifth birthday party in the middle of July—Cory having ducked her invitation by saying she would have to check her diary—the two disappeared back into the pub, leaving them alone. They were the last ones in the garden now, apart from a cheeky robin who was busy pecking a morsel of gateau under a nearby table and chasing off a horde of hopeful sparrows when they got too near his plunder.

'How long have they been married?' she asked Nick as they finished the last of their now cool coffee.

'Ten years.'

'Have they any children?'

He shifted in his seat. 'Lucinda can't have any. They tried everything but…' He shrugged. His eyes lifted to hers as he continued, 'It was a bad time. She comes from one of those huge Italian families where every daughter pops one out a year. They were living in Italy then but when she had a nervous breakdown John brought her over here for a change of scene for a while. That was five years ago and they haven't looked back since.'

'And John doesn't mind? About not having children?'

Nick looked at her levelly. 'He minds like hell, but the way he sees it he didn't fall in love with Lucinda because she was some sort of baby-making machine. He loves *her*, he always has from the day he first set eyes on her.'

Cory stared at him. She wanted to cry but he would think she was mad. Nevertheless her voice was thick when she said, 'They're lucky, the way they feel about each other, I mean.'

'Yes, they are, but they're not unique.' His eyes were holding hers now and although she wanted to break the contact she found she couldn't. 'That's what you were thinking, wasn't it,' he said softly, and it was a statement not a question. 'That they're unique. I could read it in your face.'

She wanted to deny it but he would know she was lying. 'Not unique,' she prevaricated. 'More…unusual.'

'Why do you think that way?'

It was straight for the jugular but she was recognising he was that sort of man. She couldn't answer him. She let her hair fall to cover her face. 'I don't want to continue this conversation.'

'OK.'

It was immediate and almost nonchalant and the tone shocked her. Which was ridiculous, she told herself angrily.

She hadn't wanted him to pursue the matter so why should she feel so let down that he didn't seem to care?

'Let's go for a stroll on the Heath to walk the lunch off and get ready for dinner,' Nick said easily as she raised her head again.

Dinner? Who had said anything about dinner? 'I don't think—'

'Good. Don't think. I like you better that way.'

'Now look—' And then she noticed his smile. Weakly, she said, 'You're trying to wind me up.'

'Me?' He leant forward as he stood to his feet and kissed her on the top of her nose. 'As if. Finish your wine while I go and settle with John. We'll leave the car in the pub car park for now.'

He was gone before she could object.

Cory had wanted to stay remote and detached on the Heath but she found she couldn't. The beautiful day had brought many Londoners out into the fresh air, the fathomless blue sky above too perfect to waste time indoors.

They walked hand in hand, talking now and again, and unlike in the pub garden she found herself relaxing, waves of contentment flowing over her like a balmy breeze.

'You're beginning to burn.' Nick pulled her into the shade of an old tree, the bottom of its trunk splotched with lichens and velvety moss. The grass was thick and warm as they sat down, and in the distance two young boys were throwing a Frisbee for a shaggy mutt of a dog who was barking enthusiastically as he ran.

Cory turned her head. Nick was stretched out beside her, hands clasped under his head and his eyes shut. He opened one eye. 'We've had the walk, now it's time for a nap.'

This was far too beguiling. 'You make us sound like a

couple of old-age pensioners,' she said flatly, aiming to break the mood. 'And I don't nap during the day.'

'Try.' He reached out one arm and pulled her down beside him, settling her head on his chest. 'Even a pillow provided,' he drawled lazily, idly stroking her hair. 'Now shut your eyes like a good girl.'

She was as tense as piano wire for a few minutes but then, as he made no move to kiss her or do anything except slowly stroke her hair, she found herself relaxing. The heat of the day, the dappled shade through the leaves of the tree, the muted sounds in the background all combined to unknot her nerves and make her drowsy. At the most she had only managed two or three hours' sleep the night before and the Sunday lunch had left her comfortably full, not to mention the soporific effect of the wine. She slept.

When she next opened her eyes, Nick was looking down at her. He was propped on one elbow and her head was now resting on his middle. 'Hello,' he said, very softly.

Still dazed with sleep, she murmured, 'Hallo yourself.'

When he bent and kissed her it seemed the most natural thing in the world to lift her arms about his neck. She still wasn't awake enough to fight the realisation that she had been waiting for this moment all day, the moment when he would really kiss her again.

He made no attempt to touch any other part of her body yet every nerve came alive, twanging with sensation as the kiss deepened.

When he drew away he was breathing hard, his voice gruff as he said, 'Any more and I shall forget where I am, and we don't want to frighten any little children, do we.'

She smiled as she was meant to, but she couldn't help wondering if she had imagined the note of what had sounded like surprise in his voice.

He seemed to confirm, it, however, when he said, 'I'm

not sure what you do to me, Cory James, but it could get to be like a drug.'

'Is that good or bad?' She heard herself flirt with a little stab of amazement, but it all seemed to be part of the lazy afternoon.

'Depends.' One finger traced the outline of her lips.

'On what?'

'How often I can get a fix.'

Enough. She sat up, brushing her hair out of her eyes as she said, 'I told you, I don't—'

'Date. Yes, I remember. So when do you see that changing?'

'What?'

'You'll want to settle down one day, surely, so how do you intend to find Mr Right if the opposite sex is out of bounds?' he asked smoothly.

She found his presumption galling to say the least. 'Why should I want to settle down? Because I'm a woman?'

He stared at her, the riveting blue of his eyes betraying nothing of what he was thinking. 'I've found most of your sex are inclined towards ultimate monogamy, babies, that kind of thing.'

'Well, I'm not,' she said firmly.

'You don't want babies one day?'

'No. Yes. I mean—' What did she mean? 'Babies are not part of my plans for the future.'

'That's a little harsh, isn't it?' he asked mildly.

'Not if it prevents them just being mere incidentals in someone else's life.' She'd spoken too quickly and from the heart without considering her words, and now she could have kicked herself as she watched the piercing gaze narrow.

'Incidental? Is that how you saw yourself in your parents' lives?'

Cory made a conscious effort at self-control. She couldn't believe how they had arrived at talking like this. She had known some of her friends for years and years and they had never remotely touched on such intimate subjects. She had known Nick for a couple of days and here he was giving her the third degree. 'Let's change the subject,' she said stiffly.

'Let's not.' He rose to his feet, pulling her up with him and then keeping her within the circle of his arms when she made to pull free. 'Cory, most kids grow up knowing they are the most precious things under the sun to their parents,' he said softly. 'I'm sorry, heart sorry, if it wasn't that way for you, but don't let anyone else's mistakes push you down a path where you don't really want to go.'

'How do you know where I want to go?' His words had bit into the secret recesses of her heart like acid. 'You don't know me. You didn't know my parents either so don't make any snap judgements on them or me.'

He was quite still for a moment, then he said, 'It'd be a crying shame if someone as beautiful and sensitive as you shut herself away from life. Don't you see that?'

'Life meaning sex?' she asked with a baldness that shocked her. 'And sex meaning your bed, I suppose?'

'My bed is certainly big enough to accommodate the two of us,' he said mildly, 'but I wasn't necessarily referring to it. I can actually think about something other than sex occasionally.'

'Then you're one of the few men who can.' Again she could have kicked herself, What was she *doing*? She had to calm down. He was far too perceptive for his own good—or maybe that should be *her* good. She tried to prise his arms away but they merely tightened.

'What was his name?'

'Whose name?' she hedged, swallowing hard.

'The guy who let you down. Because you have been let down by someone, haven't you, Cory? Was it recently?'

Her frozen state resembled a rabbit caught in the headlights of an oncoming car.

'You can tell me to go to hell,' he said grimly, 'but I'd rather hear if it's really over, at least from your side.'

'It's over,' she said dully.

'In your heart or in your head?'

He really didn't seem to know when to stop. The thought brought enough adrenalin for her to break free and take a step backwards, her voice a snap when she said, 'Both, OK? Both. Is that what you wanted to hear?'

'Yes, it is.' And he didn't sound in the least apologetic about his temerity.

'His name was William Patterson and he was rich, good-looking and very sure of himself. He asked me to marry him and then I found him making love to someone else. Is that enough information? Oh, and it was over three years ago now.' She had put as much sarcasm into her voice as she could to stop it trembling.

He didn't say anything for what seemed like a very long time to Cory's overwrought nerves. Then he stuffed his hands into his pockets, his eyes still on her. 'Her name was Joanna and we *were* married,' he said quietly. 'She was killed instantly when a drunk driver on the wrong side of the road knocked her car straight in front of a lorry on Christmas Eve. She'd popped out to get some bulbs for the lights on the tree so it would be ready when I walked in from work. The drunk driver had bruises, nothing else.'

'Oh, Nick.' She was scarcely breathing.

'It was a long time ago, Cory, thirteen years to be exact. We had only been left university for six months. We were still two kids, playing at being married but enjoying every moment. I was twenty-two but I grew up very quickly that night. After that…' He shrugged. 'I threw myself into work and the next year started my own business. It was good to have something to drive at.'

'And you've never… I mean, there hasn't been anyone else you've wanted to—' She stopped abruptly, aware she was putting it badly.

'I've had relationships since Joanna,' he said, 'one or two of them long-term. If you're asking me if I was ever tempted to get married again, then the answer's no.'

Cory nodded. She didn't know what to say. She'd had him down as a love 'em and leave 'em type—which he might be now—but she had to admit she hadn't thought about what might have made him that way. 'It must have been very hard for you,' she said at last.

'For a while.' He shrugged. 'But it seems like another lifetime now. The boy Joanna knew was very different to the man I've become, I guess. Who knows whether we would still even be together if she had lived? We were very young, that's for sure. And typical students. We married in a registry office one wet Saturday afternoon; she wore a long skirt and a jumper with bells round the bottom and I wore jeans and a scruffy T-shirt.'

'Bohemians.'

'Something like that.' He smiled at her, reaching out and taking her hand, and she let him pull her into his side as they began walking again.

Even as she was making all the right noises, Cory found her mind was working on a different plane altogether as they strolled back to the pub. Nick Morgan was inveigling himself into her life somehow, and it frightened her. She was sure he hadn't made up the story about his young wife, but had he told her about Joanna hoping it would soften her attitude to him? William had been full of little tricks like that. In fact, once their relationship was over she'd realised William had played her like a master virtuoso. She frowned to herself.

'You're thinking again.' The deep voice was amused.

'What?' She wiped her face clear of expression as she glanced up at him.

'I'd bet a pound to a penny I was featuring in your thoughts and not favourably,' he drawled. 'Right?'

'Don't be ridiculous.' She could feel her cheeks burning. 'Something along the lines of wondering if I'd spun you a yarn, yes?'

'No.' Her voice carried a note of indignation that couldn't be misconstrued. 'Of course I believe what you told me. I know you wouldn't make something like that up.' Even as she spoke Cory wondered how she knew. But know she did. She decided to look at that one later.

'Then you're wondering *why* I told you,' he persisted doggedly.

Wretched man. She turned her head, pretending an interest in two screaming toddlers whose harassed mother was trying to persuade them back into a double buggy. 'I don't know what you're talking about.'

'Little liar.' It was soft, indulgent, and took the sting out of the words.

Cory decided she could do some plain speaking herself. She stopped, looking up into the clear blue eyes as she said, 'OK then, why *did* you tell me?'

'I don't know.' He didn't blink, his face oddly vulnerable. Cory didn't like what it did to her treacherous heart. Then, with a wry smile, he said, 'It's not something I usually drop into the conversation on the second date. In fact it's not something I usually talk about at all.'

How could someone who was so big and male and dangerous look so boyish for a moment? She told herself she'd had enough of aching heartstrings for one afternoon and answered his smile with one of her own, saying lightly, 'Looks like we're both in the dark then. And we're not dating, remember? This is my penance.'

He chuckled and her heart thudded with pleasure that she could make him laugh, even as a hundred alarm bells went off in her head. He was the most exciting man she had ever met, she'd known that yesterday, but today she'd realised there was much more to Nick than met the eye. He probably had a lighthearted little romance in mind, a few romps in bed until the next woman came along, a woman more suited to his complex and captivating personality. But she wasn't *like* that.

They walked on, the warm evening air redolent of woodsmoke from a distant bonfire somewhere, but Cory's mind was racing.

How did you tell an experienced man of the world like Nick Morgan, a man who by his own admission had had more than one woman in his bed in his time—lots more—that you had never actually...

She groaned inwardly. He would laugh at her and somehow—somehow she couldn't bear the thought of that.

Of course she had had her moments in the days before she had tangled with William. Her friends at university had been popping in and out of bed with the current boyfriend as though it was as simple and easy as having a cup of tea. They had said she was too intense, that she was making too big a deal out of what was the most natural thing in the world, but something had always stopped her from making total bodily commitment with the lads she had gone out with.

She supposed she'd been waiting for the Mr Right Nick had spoken of earlier. Her lip curled at her naïvety. Even though she'd always doubted anyone would feel that way about her in her heart.

They reached the pub within a few minutes and after saying their goodbyes to Lucinda and John walked to the car. As they drove back along the route they had travelled earlier, Cory said tentatively, 'I brought some work home I really ought to look at before tomorrow. If you wouldn't mind dropping me back at the flat now, please.'

'I do mind.' He spared her one piercing glance before going on, 'We're doing dinner, Cory. Relax and you might even enjoy it.'

She wriggled in her seat. 'Where are we going?'

'A nice little place I know.'

'You know so many nice little places,' she said with a touch of acidity.

He chose to ignore it. 'That's true, but this one is special. Trust me.'

That would be a grave mistake.

Her face must have spoken for itself because she became aware of him laughing softly, and when she looked at him his eyes were brilliant with sparks of humour. 'You're priceless,' he murmured. 'Do you know that? And so good for keeping my ego on the ground.'

'I don't think I'll feel sorry for your ego,' she said, thinking of all the other women he had said he'd known and feeling ridiculously jealous. Which just showed how crazy she was and how this had to be the end of things.

The light banter continued as they drove on, but when they drew up in one of the streets close to Richmond Park Cory stared about her. 'This isn't a restaurant,' she said accusingly.

'Who said anything about a restaurant?' Twilight was beginning to fall as he slid out of the car, walking round the sleek low bonnet and opening her door for her.

Cory remained sitting. She raised her eyebrows at him

and he stared innocently back. 'So?' she said meaningfully. 'Where are we?'

'Outside my London flat.'

She'd already arrived at that conclusion herself but had been determined to make him spell it out. She opened her mouth to tell him to take her home but he forestalled her.

'Before you say anything, it's only dinner that's on the cards, by the way. I know you'd like to get your hands on my body but you'll just have to restrain yourself.'

Cory glared at him. 'This isn't funny, Nick.'

He crouched down so that his head was on a level with hers. She tried hard to ignore the way his trousers strained over muscled thighs but it was difficult. 'Only dinner, Cory,' he repeated softly. 'I thought it would be nice to eat in, that's all. That way I can enjoy a bottle of wine with you and call a taxi to take you home.'

'You can cook?' she asked doubtfully.

'My dumplings have been known to make women swoon.'

She giggled, she couldn't help it. 'Really, *can* you cook?' she persisted.

He smiled. 'Tonight we're starting with spiced chicken salad with papaya and avocado. I cheated and got that ready before I left this morning. The main course for madam is pork and ginger stir-fry with noodles and prawn crackers. And for dessert…'

'What's for dessert?' Her mouth was watering.

'That'll be a surprise.' He stood up again, holding out his hand which she took a little reluctantly, still unsure of what she was doing.

Once she was standing on the pavement she eyed him warily. He was certainly full of surprises, and she didn't mean the dessert! Who on earth would have guessed he could cook? He was too...male. And then she couldn't believe she'd been so sexist.

'Come on.' He led her over to the large terraced house in front of them. As soon as he opened the front door Cory knew his flat was going to be sumptuous by the splendour of the marbled lobby complete with lift.

Nick's flat was at the top of the house and, when he stood aside for her to enter after opening the front door, Cory looked about her interestedly. She saw immediately that she had been right. It *was* sumptuous, but not overpoweringly so. It was also severely male, no frills or fancies littering the contemporary feel of the flat.

The lounge area which opened from the front door had pale cream walls and an oatmeal carpet, the huge sensation of space enhanced by the absence of doors between it and the dining room. The designer had left the chimney breast only as a natural division, and Cory could see by the charred logs in the grate that this was a real fire.

Three black leather two-seater sofas and several black lacquer oval occasional tables dotted the lounge, and in the dining room the monochrome effect continued with a black dining table and chairs.

Several striking pieces of sculpture and bark wall hangings and a row of steel-framed mirrors added to the air of uncompromising stark beauty. There were no plants, no ornaments, no vases of flowers or photographs on view, nothing to give any idea of the personality of the man who owned the place.

Cory turned to look at Nick, who was watching her intently. 'Is your house in Barnstaple like this?'

The hard face relaxed into a smile. 'No,' he admitted softly, 'but that's home. This is part of my work. It's where I bring colleagues, clients, people I want to impress.'

Cory nodded. She knew his international electronics firm

was huge and still growing. He was a very successful and intelligent man and she supposed this flat reflected this. She wouldn't want to live in it though.

'Come through to the kitchen,' Nick said, the twist to his lips suggesting he had read her mind again. 'It's where I spend most of my time when I'm here, that and the bed-room. I tend to get in late and leave early unless I'm en-tertaining.'

The kitchen was a smart combination of brushed stain-less steel and solid wedge wood, and the impression of space and light was continued here by the ceiling having been removed, revealing the timbers of the original struc-ture which were painted white. A large corner breakfast bar which was really a small table had two high stainless steel chairs with coffee-coloured upholstered seats tucked be-neath it and, after pulling one out, Nick said, 'Sit down while I see about dinner. I'll open a bottle of wine. A nice Chardonnay, I think, to go with the salad and then the stir-fry.'

She had half been expecting that he would give her a tour of all of the flat, including his bedroom, and now as she sat on the chair she had to confess to a slight feeling of disappointment. She would have liked to see where he slept, to be able to picture him there at night. *Dangerous.* The word reverberated in her head as loudly as if someone had screamed it in her ear. She didn't need to picture him anywhere; he had no part in her life. This was one weekend out of the norm and it would remain like that. A pleasant but acutely disturbing episode that would soon fade from her memory if she put her mind to it.

Oh, yeah? challenged a little voice in her head. And pigs might fly.

The Chardonnay was as delicious in its own way as the Brunello at lunch. Cory didn't know much about different wines but it was obvious Nick did. All part of the image, she told herself, before feeling a little ashamed of the cattiness which had prompted the thought.

'Can I help?' she asked as she sat watching him deftly cut the pork loin into thin strips before covering it and putting it with the other ingredients he'd pulled out of the fridge, already prepared for cooking—a man who thought of everything.

He took a swallow of his wine before saying, 'You could set two places in the dining room if you like.'

'We're not eating in here?' The dining room table was enormous for two, besides which the informality of the kitchen was less conducive to a romantic tête-à-tête, surrounded as they were by gleaming pans and kitchen utensils.

'Is that what you'd prefer?' And, as she nodded, he said, 'So be it. Cutlery and everything else you'll need is in the cupboard to your left.'

They ate the first course almost immediately and it was truly delicious. Nick seemed determined to be the perfect host, making her laugh with one amusing story after another and displaying none of the intuitive and disconcerting probing which had so bothered her during the afternoon.

He wouldn't let her help with the main course, so Cory sat sipping her wine as she watched him cook the pork strips until they were brown all over, at which point he added the garlic, ginger, spring onions, pineapple chunks and other ingredients.

He was perfectly relaxed and at ease in the kitchen, adding the oyster sauce to the stir-fry with one hand and dealing with the noodles and prawn crackers with the other, whilst talking of inconsequential things. Cory could only marvel at him. She wasn't too bad a cook when she put her mind to it, but she didn't particularly like an audience and certainly couldn't have coped with Nick watching *her*.

Cory ate the ginger and pork stir-fry in a delicious haze of well-being, only protesting very slightly when Nick re-filled her empty glass. 'This food is so *good*,' she said, wrapping a noodle round her fork and transferring it to her mouth. 'I can't make my meals taste like this.'

He smiled lazily. 'The secret is in using fresh ingredients, like the root ginger and garlic. I never buy my herbs and spices in packets.'

Cory gave a hiccup of a laugh and then put down her glass of wine which she had just picked up. She suddenly realised she'd had quite enough. It was deceptively potent stuff.

'What's funny?' he asked softly.

She tried very hard to pull herself together. 'Just that I never imagined we'd be discussing the pros and cons of herbs and spices,' she said in a voice which was shaky with the amusement she was trying to quell. 'You didn't strike me as that sort of man when I met you, that's all.'

'What sort of man did you think I was then?' he asked lightly.

Cory considered her answer, forgetting she wasn't going to drink any more wine and taking several sips as she surveyed him through dreamy eyes. 'A he-man type,' she stated.

'And they don't cook?'

'I don't know.' Wrapped in contentment and lulled into a false sense of security she forgot to be careful. 'They might do. You do, so other men might, I suppose.'

'What about William?' Nick asked softly. 'Didn't he spoil you by at least cooking breakfast now and again?'

'I never had breakfast with William. I've never had breakfast with anyone.' She finished the last of the wine, holding out her glass for a refill as she spoke out the thought in her head without thinking about what she was revealing. 'I suppose you have to sleep with someone to wake up to breakfast with them.'

There was the merest of pauses before Nick said, 'It helps.'

There was a quality to his voice which brought Cory back to earth more effectively than a bucketful of cold water.

Much later she realised that at that point she could still have saved the situation if she hadn't lost her head. She could have made some light innuendo which suggested that bed wasn't the only place people made love or deflected the assumption she had heard in his voice in some other way. Then maybe—*maybe*—she might have fooled him.

As it was, she stared at him with wide horrified eyes, the effects of the wine completely burnt up in the mortification she was feeling. She set the wineglass down on the table. 'Not that I haven't had lots of offers though,' she blurted out before realising that made everything ten times worse.

Jumping to her feet she took the coward's way out. 'Can I use the bathroom?'

'Sure.' Nick was magnificently unconcerned but it didn't help. 'First door on your right outside the kitchen.'

Cory fled.

She stood in the bathroom for a good few seconds feeling utterly wretched before her surroundings registered through the maelstrom. Then she glanced about her in awe. The white tiled walls and floor were offset with midnight-blue granite surfaces and illuminated recesses which stored white bath-linen and toiletries, and the massive raised bath, shower cubicle, pedestal basin, toilet and bidet were white with elegant silver fittings. Two exquisitely worked granite sculptures of storks stood either side of the shower cubicle, a mosaic of white and blue taking up almost one wall over the bath.

The stark use of white and blue, the voyeuristic ceiling which consisted totally of glass and the carefully positioned lighting made this a bathroom where modesty would go out of the window. Cory walked gingerly across to the basin, fiddling about for a few moments before she realised it had a thermostat mixer and sensor which was activated when the occupant held their hands beneath it.

But of course it would, she told herself cantankerously. What else? She wouldn't be surprised if you only had to wish for the bath to fill up and it happened.

She glanced up at the ceiling again when she had dried her hands on the big fluffy towel and then her eyes moved to the huge bath which would easily take two people, if not a whole rugby team. This room had been designed for other activities than merely getting clean. She put her hands to her hot cheeks. Which made what she'd revealed to Nick doubly humiliating. He wouldn't have any concept of how she felt.

She stayed in the bathroom for as long as she dared but eventually she squared her shoulders and lifted her head. She would have to go and face him and get it over with. She breathed very deeply. But definitely no more wine. No more wine, no more leading conversations, no more of anything!

He was sitting where she'd left him, but now their plates had been cleared away and dessert dishes and spoons were on the table. 'Hi.' His smile was easy and unhurried as she joined him. 'Vanilla parfait with chocolate rum truffle or apricot whisky mousse?'

Cory forgot to be embarrassed as she stared at the two rich concoctions in front of her. 'You made these?' she asked in amazement.

'Almost.' His eyes drifted over her face. 'But my local gourmet store helped a little.'

Her smiled was strained. She didn't want to eat dessert with him in this gleaming super-technological kitchen. She wanted to go home and lick her wounds.

As soon as she had finished her portion of vanilla parfait with chocolate rum truffle, Cory slipped off her seat. 'I must go home and do that work,' she said quietly. 'Thanks for a lovely day. I'll hail a cab from the end of the street.'

'Don't be silly, I'm coming with you.'

'There's no need.'

He inhaled deeply and audibly, and let his breath out. 'I'm coming with you,' he repeated steadily, rising to his feet.

His tone was exactly what one would use with a difficult and annoying child, and it caught her on the raw. She stared at him and piercingly intent blue eyes stared back. He seemed very big and very dark and Cory couldn't help looking at his mouth as he stopped speaking. It was a sexy, cynical and purposeful mouth. She swallowed. 'As you like,' she said casually, shrugging as she turned away.

The next moment she was turned around again by a firm hand on her shoulder. 'I do like,' he said with silky control. He put his mouth to hers, stroking her sealed lips as one hand held her in the small of her back and the other brushed her hair away from her face.

When her lips opened slightly beneath his he plunged immediately into the undefended territory, his hand leaving her face to thread deftly into her hair, supporting her head. The kiss deepened with a sensuality that started her senses reeling.

'You're delicious, you know that, don't you,' he murmured, a sound—almost like a groan—coming from deep in his throat. 'Specially tasting of rum truffle.'

The hand that had been tangled in her hair had shifted to fit her face into the curve of his neck and now he stood cradling her close, so close she could feel every inch of his arousal. Cory stood absolutely still. She was having trouble with her breathing and her heart was pounding. The overpowering passion which ignited every time this man touched her had taken her unawares again, and now all her doubts and fears came back in a rush to reproach her.

Act nonchalant, she told herself silently. Finish this with a modicum of self-respect. If nothing else, let him remember you as the one who got away.

She straightened, pulling away and smoothing her hair with a light laugh before she said, 'Red wine, white wine and now rum truffle. You're a bad influence.'

'I hope so.' The unreserved warmth in his eyes brought colour into her cheeks, especially as the feel of his body was still imprinted against her. 'But we've a long way to go yet.'

Cory looked at him guardedly but made no reply. The only place she was going was home, and then from this night on she'd make sure she refused any invitations from Nick Morgan. If he asked her to see him again, that was. She ignored the chasm that her stomach had fallen into at the thought of never seeing him again, and said brightly, 'Shall we find a taxi now?'

'Let's.' It was dry.

They didn't say much on the way to Cory's flat, but the air in the back of the taxi was electric with tension. At least, Cory felt so. Nick, on the other hand, sat with his arm round her, the hand resting on her shoulder playing idly with a lock of her hair and his legs stretched out lazily in front of him.

His kisses didn't mean anything. The refrain went over

and over in her head as she tried to convince herself. Not a thing. To a man like Nick, kissing a woman was little more than a social habit.

Why had he stopped kissing her? The thought which had assailed her as they had left his flat kept jabbing at her. Because it hadn't been her who had stopped initially. It *should* have been, she acknowledged miserably, but it hadn't. Was it because of what she'd unwittingly revealed? Had it put him off? Did he feel he couldn't be bothered with someone as inexperienced as her? Or perhaps, like her friends at university, he thought she was too intense, too emotional—slightly...odd?

She continued to go round and round in circles until the car drew up outside the house and then, to her surprise, she had a feeling of very real panic at the thought of not seeing him again. Which was ridiculous, utterly and absolutely. Nevertheless it was there.

'I'll see you to your door,' Nick said, and this time she didn't object. He told the taxi driver to wait and then escorted her across the pavement, following her inside the house after she had opened the front door.

When they were finally standing outside her own door, she looked up at him. How had he managed to become such a part of her life in two days? It was scary. So, so scary.

'Don't look at me like that,' he said roughly.

'Like what?' she asked, genuinely hurt by the thread of anger.

'Like you expect me to treat you badly, manhandle you, hurt you.'

She supposed she did expect him to hurt her if she got involved with him, but not in the physical sense he was talking about.

'*Hell*, Cory.' He was suddenly furious and it showed.

'Give me a break, won't you. I don't know how this William guy behaved but I'm not him. OK? It might be stating the obvious but I need to say it.'

'I know you're not him,' she said shakily.

'Do you? I don't think you do, not yet.' And then he echoed her earlier thought when he said, 'It's been two days and yet it feels like much, much longer. Do you feel that?'

She wanted to make some clever, witty comment and then send him on his way, or even just shake her head. She nodded instead.

'Do you see the age gap as a problem?'

'What?' It had been the last thing she'd expected him to say.

'I'm ten years older than you. Does that bother you?' he asked softly.

She didn't know what to say. Something was happening here and she seemed to have no control over it. She shook her head because she couldn't have spoken to save her life.

'You're going to tell me we inhabit different worlds, aren't you?' he went on.

She hadn't been but now he'd mentioned it it was absolutely true.

'And you're right,' he said quietly. 'For the last thirteen years I've worked like a dog and loved every minute, and any woman I've got involved with has known the score. At first I was so cut up about Joanna it was easier to keep relationships from developing into anything but physical ones. There are plenty of career women out there who aren't looking to settle down until way on in their timescale of things, and they suited me as I did them. Fun, friendship, someone warm in bed but no emotional commitment. Then, as time went on, I found I was becoming autonomous because I *liked* it that way, not because of any lingering loyalty to Joanna. The freedom of being self-determining and independent was heady.'

She stared at him, her eyes wide. Was he being brutally honest at last? Was he going to say that any relationship with him would be purely physical and only last as long as he wanted it to? His other women had obviously been happy with that.

And then he disabused her of that idea. 'You might be a career woman but you aren't like them, are you.' It was a statement, not a question. 'You think differently.'

This was all because of what she had inadvertently told him before dessert. That she was a virgin. A twenty-five-year-old virgin. Was this his way of telling her he wasn't going to see her again because she wasn't like the other women, wasn't what he wanted?

Her chin rose a notch. 'Nick,' she began, but he put a finger to her lips.

'We come from different ends of the pole, Cory, but you know as well as I do that there's a spark there. It's there when I touch you and it's there when I don't. And I like that. It makes me feel alive,' he added wryly. 'I didn't realise till I met you that I was growing stale. So, how about we see each other once in a while, take it nice and easy and see how things go? Sure there'll be hurdles, but we'll take them one at a time and see what happens. What do you say?'

Every single brain cell was telling her to say no. It was the sensible, the *safe* thing to do. She had been this way once before with William and it had ended in disaster. This would too. She knew it at heart. Nick would grow bored with her; it was inevitable with a man like him. No was the only answer to give.

But she couldn't do it. She couldn't tell him to walk away from her. Not yet.

Cory was unaware of the play of emotions across her face, but when he pulled her to him she realised he'd guessed something of what she was feeling. 'So, do we start doing the dreaded "d" word?' he asked drily.

She looked into the blue eyes. From somewhere she found the strength to be as cool and laid-back as him. 'I guess we'd better give it a shot for a while,' she said airily. 'If only to stop you growing stale.'

CHAPTER FIVE

'OH, DARLING, that's absolutely wonderful. I'm so pleased. Haven't I said you need another boyfriend, if only to spite William?'

Cory smiled at her aunt. For someone who had lived most of her adult life in the crazy and often promiscuous world of fashion, Joan could be terribly ingenuous. 'For one thing, Nick's not my boyfriend,' she said gently, not wanting to disappoint the older woman. 'We're just going to date sometimes, that's all. And, considering I haven't seen William for three years, I doubt very much if anything I do would affect him in the slightest. He didn't care when we were together as he proved only too well. He'd hardly take any interest now.'

'What do you mean, he's not your boyfriend?' said Joan, ignoring the rest. 'You said Nick wants to see you. It's not one of these modern open sort of things, is it? Where he can do what he likes and so can you?'

'Not exactly.' To be truthful, she wasn't sure what it was, but she couldn't very well say that.

'I'd like to meet him,' stated Joan definitely.

Cory's nerves jangled. Joan had only met William once and it had been such an unmitigated disaster that they hadn't repeated it. 'I've only seen him twice myself,' she objected. 'I can hardly ask him round for an inspection by you.'

'Not an inspection.' Joan fixed her with a look that said she wasn't about to be deflected. 'Just to dinner.'

'Not yet,' Cory said firmly. Maybe not at all. She was

due to go out to the theatre with him in the middle of the week and she was preparing herself already for the possibility that things might have changed between them. The weekend they had just shared had been...good—she wouldn't allow herself a more enthusiastic summing up—but they might meet again and there would be nothing there. For him at least. And that would be fine, it *would*. She was expecting nothing from this relationship that wasn't really a relationship at all. She was *ordinary*, for crying out loud.

She had spent most of the day in the house of a family who hadn't a clue about personal hygiene or the most elementary social graces, trying to ascertain if the children were neglected out of intent or simply because their young parents didn't have a clue.

She had returned home exhausted and stinking of the smell peculiar to the Massey family—a mixture of cat's urine, dirt, cooking smells and body odour—which permeated every nook and cranny and ingrained itself into clothes, hair and nails. After washing her hair and having a long, hot bath she had gone round to her aunt's house for dinner as she did every Monday, only to find that the odour seemed to have lodged itself somewhere between the end of her nose and her brain.

She could just imagine Nick's reaction if he had seen her earlier. She almost laughed to herself. Nick, with his incredible flat, cars, designer clothes and immaculate appearance. No, they were miles, tens of thousands of miles apart. It was never going to come to anything. He was like a bright shooting star and she was like a damp squib.

'Not yet?' Joan was the original British bulldog when she wanted to be. 'When then? Now your parents are gone I feel responsible for you.'

Now Cory did laugh out loud. 'You know as well as I

do that Mum and Dad barely knew I was alive,' she said, just the merest trace of bitterness showing through. 'And they would never have claimed to be responsible for me.'

'Their loss.' Joan sighed, looking into the lovely young face opposite her and wondering how two intelligent people like Cory's parents could have been so criminally blind to their own daughter's needs. 'But I do worry about you. I can't help it. And I know you are a perfectly modern woman who is in control of her life and her destiny, but still...'

Cory wasn't at all sure about the control bit. 'Maybe in a couple of months,' she said placatingly. If they were still seeing each other then. Which she doubted. The tug at her heartstrings which followed was worrying.

'I shall keep you to that,' Joan said with great satisfaction. 'Now, have a piece of the shortbread I made this afternoon with your coffee. I'm really getting the hang of this cooking lark, aren't I, Rufus,' she added to the dog sitting drooling at her feet. 'After all those years at work when I ate out or had a ready meal in front of the TV, I've found it's very satisfying to start a meal from scratch with fresh ingredients.'

'You and Nick are going to have a lot to talk about,' said Cory wryly.

They did. Two months later—months in which she and Nick had seen each other almost every night—Cory found herself watching him charm his way into her aunt's affections. He had arrived at the house with a vast collection of herbs, all in little plant pots—'thought it'd go down better than a bunch of flowers', he'd murmured to Cory, who'd arrived early to help her aunt with the dinner—and an enormous hide bone for Rufus. The dog had promptly claimed Nick as his own personal companion, sitting on his foot all through dinner and then plonking himself down at the side of Nick's armchair when they'd retired to Joan's conservatory overlooking her pretty little garden.

The doors had been open to the warm August evening and in the distance somebody had been cutting their lawn, the drone of the lawnmower soothing. When Nick and her aunt had begun an in-depth conversation concerning the merits of certain herbs in certain dishes and other gastronomic delights, Cory had found herself beginning to doze. She'd had a hard week with a particularly harrowing case, and now the big meal, comfortable chair, mellow evening sunshine and general sense of well-being was seductive.

She was woken by a lingering kiss on her lips. She opened her eyes to find her aunt was nowhere to be seen. 'Where's she gone?' she asked Nick drowsily.

'Your aunt? Taken Rufus for a quick walk in the park. Apparently they have a little routine at nights now her leg's better. Rufus has a chance to meet Oscar—an Old English Sheepdog,' Nick explained knowledgeably, 'and Periwinkle—a German Shepherd. According to your aunt, they are the canine version of the Three Musketeers and Rufus is bereft if they don't meet up.' His expression changed. 'Were you bored earlier?' he asked softly.

'Bored?' She gazed into the hard handsome face and wondered if he was aware of how devastatingly gorgeous he was. 'How could anyone be bored listening to the merits of basil and thyme, or curd cheese over butter icing?'

He was used to her chaffing him. She had decided in the very early days that the only way she was going to hold her own in this relationship was not to fall foul of his charm.

He grinned at her now and she caught her breath as the blue eyes crinkled sexily at the corners. 'Worked though, didn't it,' he said with a great deal of satisfaction. 'Your aunt is putty in my hands.'

So was she but she wasn't about to let him know that. 'I'll set her straight another time,' she promised drily.

'Come here.' His voice had changed and as she stood up he pulled her into his arms, his tone husky as he said, 'I've been wanting to do this all evening.' His kiss was fierce, hungry, and she matched him in fierceness and hunger. It was always like that. And she knew the day was fast approaching when he would want it all, want her in his bed. She wanted it too. It had never been that way with William. Nothing was as it had been with William. That ought to be comforting but it wasn't because she just couldn't bring herself to believe that the bubble wouldn't burst.

They stood moulded together and swaying slightly as their hands explored each other while their mouths fused. Nick nipped and sipped and savoured the sweet taste of her, pressing the tip of his tongue against her throat where her pulse pounded in reaction. He knew just what buttons to press, exactly how to please her. She knew going to bed with this man would be an experience she'd never get over. She would be his slave for ever.

'Pity your aunt's going to be back any minute.' Reluctantly he raised his head, his voice husky as he adjusted her clothing.

His eyes had turned a deeper blue than usual and she smiled at him, the thrill she always felt at knowing how much he wanted her sending little ripples down her spine.

'I want you, Cory.' He ran one fingertip down her throat and into the dip between her breasts and she shivered. 'And you want me. Not in little snatched moments or an evening here and there.'

Wanting was dangerous. Needing even more so. She

stared at him, her eyes enormous in the shadows which were encroaching as night fell.

'I love you,' he said very softly. 'Do you love me?'

She had known it would come to this one day. The summer had been so wonderful, so magical, but underlying every day had been a complicated web which had got stickier the more they had been together. The gap between them was as immense as it had ever been. He spoke of love but what he really meant was that he wanted her. Not just physically, she knew he wasn't as crass as William and that he enjoyed being with her, but as for it lasting...

She drew back a little in his arms as she looked up at him. She had to be honest here. It was the only way but she was frightened this would be the moment he would get tired of her. 'I'm not sure I know what love is,' she said carefully. 'My parents had this feeling between them they said was love but to me, on the outside, it was more of an obsession. It made them cruel to...to other people without them even knowing it.'

'To you?' he murmured, retaining her in his hold, his eyes narrowed on her face which was pale with emotion.

She nodded. 'One of my flatmates at university said I'd been programmed from birth to accept the fact I was unloveable and unworthy. I hated her for it at the time—she wasn't a particularly good friend and was always analysing everyone because she was doing psychology—but she might have been right. She said because I'd never experienced love when I was young—the old thing of give me a child until he's seven and I will give you the man—I'd never know it in my adult life.'

Nick swore, just once but so explicitly Cory was shocked. 'Get that out of your head,' he said roughly. 'That's rubbish and the woman wants locking away.'

'She got a First.'

'She'd get a darn sight more if I got my hands on her.'
He shook her gently. 'Listen to me, Cory. Life is what you
make of it, OK? You don't play with the cards you would
have liked, you play with the ones you've been dealt and
some of them can be lousy. Look at Lucinda. The woman
was built to have babies—big, fat, Italian babies—but can
you honestly say she is grieving her life away? Look at her
at her birthday party; she was happy and making the most
of what she *did* have.'

They had had a whale of a time at the party, which had
gone on all night until everyone had been served breakfast,
but now Cory said, 'She knows John loves her, really loves
her, and she loves him. She's not confused or inhibited.
She trusts him.'

'Dead right. But if they could have had children their
love would have flowed over and encompassed each one.
You see that, don't you? Because it's real, it's not selfish
or restricting. You said yourself what your parents had was
more obsession than love, so how the hell can you weigh
anything they said or did to you in the balance and find
yourself wanting? Of course you're loveable. Damn it, I
could eat you alive.'

She didn't return his smile. How could she explain to
him that she knew deep inside the day would come when
he didn't want her any more? She didn't have the power
to inspire real love. If she didn't have it for her parents then
why would anyone else love her? 'William said he loved
me,' she said flatly.

'William was a piece of dirt.'

She raised tortured eyes to his. 'You can't say that. You
have never even met him.'

'Let's hope I don't, for his sake,' Nick said grimly.
'Cory, the guy was on the make and he strung you along.

There are men like that out there but we're not all the same. I have never lied to you and I never will.'

No, but that wouldn't make it any the easier when he got tired of her. He could have any woman he liked. Why on earth would he stay with her?

'You think if you let yourself love me I'll treat you like William, right?'

She could tell he was struggling to remain calm and she couldn't blame him. She wished he would let go of her. She couldn't think clearly when he was holding her. She shook her head. 'I've told you, I don't think you're like him. Maybe at first, but not when I got to know you.'

'So where is the problem, for crying out loud?'

Me. I'm the problem.

The sudden arrival of Rufus shooting through to the conservatory followed by Joan calling out she was back brought the very unsatisfactory conversation to a close. Cory got her wish because Nick let go of her, bending down to stroke the dog as Joan came bustling through.

'Sorry we've been a while but Rufus is so popular it's always difficult to get away,' she said, for all the world as though she'd been accompanying a sought after celebrity to some event or other. 'Now, coffee, yes? And you must try one of my demerara meringues, Nick. They don't have the cloying sweetness of meringues made with white sugar. Have you ever tried your hand at meringues?'

Cory made an excuse and left them to it. When she reached her aunt's neat pink and cream bathroom she locked the door behind her and sank down on the edge of the bath. She was trembling and she didn't seem able to stop. He had said he loved her but he'd probably said the same thing to the women he'd had long-term relationships with in the past. Love didn't necessarily equate to staying

together or fidelity or dependability or any of those sorts
of things.

She ran her hand through her hair before groaning softly.
Was she being too possessive and clingy here? Thousands
of women the whole world over were quite happy to give
themselves body and soul to a man without the promise
that it was going to work out, or even that they would stay
together for more than a short while. If things went wrong
they picked themselves up, brushed themselves down and
got on with their lives. She worked with women like that
and there had been plenty among her friends at university.
Strong, determined, independent women.

She got up and walked over to her aunt's basin, washing
her hands with a rather strong-smelling lavender soap before drying them on a rose-embroidered towel, her head
buzzing.

When William left her life so unpleasantly she hadn't
crumbled. She might have been crying inside but she'd gritted her teeth and presented the normal capable Cory to the
rest of the world. Only her aunt had understood what his
betrayal had meant to her. Of course she hadn't given herself wholeheartedly to William, not in mind or body. But
if she stayed with Nick she would do that.

She raised her head and stared at the wide-eyed girl in
the mirror. *Because she loved him*, she thought sickly, facing it for the first time. She had been lying to him downstairs. She knew what love was since Nick had come into
her life, and the affection she had felt for William before
he had hurt her was a pale reflection in comparison. Her
pride and fragile self-esteem had been hurt when William
had treated her so badly but her heart hadn't been broken.

She sank down on the edge of the bath again, staring at
the rose tiles without really seeing them. Right, she thought
grimly. Where did she go from here? If she went into this

for real it would involve staying at his place and him at hers, that much had been clear from what he'd said downstairs about not wanting her in little snatched moments or the odd evening. It might even involve them living together. How would she survive if—when—it finished?

A coldness invaded her limbs in spite of the warm August night and she shivered. What sort of heartache would she be letting herself in for? How would she pick up the pieces and carry on? True, she'd have her work. Somehow that was supremely unimportant. And her friends and Aunt Joan. Not even in the equation.

She squeezed her lids tightly shut and tried to *think*. She was afraid to care and afraid to be cared for. That was what it boiled down to. Nick would expect that she would trust him and she would, in so far as other women were concerned. He wouldn't play the field when he was with her; he wasn't like that. But if he fell out of love with her and in love with one of the glamorous, exciting businesswomen he met every day…

She took a long shaky breath. And she couldn't expect anything else to happen long-term, not realistically. He had made it clear when they first met that his work was his life and women fitted into the niche he'd allowed for them. He needed his independence, he'd said, had found he liked autonomy, no complications in his love life.

An increase of pressure from somewhere inside her chest made it difficult for her to breathe. She had known from the beginning that she should have sent him packing after that first weekend. But she had miscalculated. She had thought it was Nick who was dangerous but in fact it had been her own feelings that were the real hazard. From the first time she'd met him she had known she could love him. But she had been too cowardly to face that then and do something about it. And now everything was a million times worse.

She couldn't be what he wanted. She rose and began pacing back and forth. And that was it in a nutshell really. She wouldn't be able to let him go gracefully when the time came; in fact, she wouldn't be able to let him go at all. And then it would all turn horribly messy and nasty. It happened, all the time.

But not to her. She stopped the pacing and became very still. Because she wouldn't let it. This was the point where she had to take control. OK, it was hellishly late in the day but better late than never. She smiled bleakly.

Nick and her aunt were sitting eating demerara meringues and drinking coffee when she joined them.

'Excuse us starting, darling, but you were such a long time.' Joan gazed up at her, her smile changing to a frown of concern. 'Are you all right, Cory? You look terribly pale all of a sudden.'

'I have a headache.' It was true, she did. Her head was pounding fit to burst.

'Oh, I'm sorry, sweetie.' Her aunt jumped up. 'I'll get some aspirin.'

When Joan had disappeared into the house, Nick leant across and took one of her hands. 'You're cold,' he said quietly. 'You must be sickening for something. Do you want me to take you home?'

What she wanted was to turn the clock back to the time before she had met him. A time in which there had been no crazy highs and lows, just a steady calm stroll through life. She nodded, wincing as the movement sent pain shooting through her eyeballs. A migraine. She hadn't had one of these in years.

By the time she had swallowed the aspirin and they had

made their goodbyes, bright lights were flashing at the back of her eyeballs. Cory knew the signs. She had had a series of migraines at university which the doctor there had put down to excess stress. She would be nauseous soon; she could feel her stomach beginning to churn already.

She stumbled as Nick helped her into the car and didn't protest when he fastened her seat belt for her. He could have stripped her stark naked and she wouldn't have cared.

'You need a doctor.' His voice sounded so loud he could have been shouting, her hearing sensitised a hundredfold.

'It's just a migraine,' she whispered through numb lips, praying she wouldn't vomit all over his beautiful car.

'Do you have them often?'

The engine was such that it fairly purred but tonight it resembled a jet preparing for take-off. 'No, not often.' Please don't make me talk.

He must have heard the silent plea because he said no more, pulling out of her aunt's drive and into the road beyond slowly and smoothly.

Even in the midst of the pain Cory appreciated his thoughtfulness. Slow was not normally a word which featured in Nick's driving vocabulary.

When they reached her flat Cory just had time to dive into the bathroom where she lost Joan's delicious plaice florentine down the toilet. She was vaguely aware of Nick helping her to her feet and then using a wet flannel to mop her face. 'I'll be fine, now, thanks,' she whispered painfully. 'I'm only ever sick once. I shall just go to bed and stay there for twenty-four hours.'

He made no reply to this, taking her arm and leading her through to her bedroom as though she was a frail old lady. Mind you, that was exactly what she felt like right at this moment, Cory thought painfully.

Once she was sitting on her bed, she said again, 'I'll be fine now. You go.'

'You're far from fine and I'm not convinced this is a migraine. What if you've got food poisoning or something?'

'Aunt Joan would love to hear you say that.'

'Not through her cooking; your aunt and I aren't affected. What did you eat for lunch?'

She really didn't want to do this right now. Forcing herself to reply, Cory murmured, 'Tagliatelle and it was perfectly all right. I've told you, this is a migraine. Now, if you don't mind, I want to go to bed.'

'Fine. I'll help you. Where's your nightie or whatever you wear?'

Cory opened one eye and then wished she hadn't as the equivalent of a laser blast hit her brain. 'I'm quite capable of undressing myself,' she said irritably, wincing as her voice added to the drums beating in her head. 'Now, if you'll just go and leave me alone so I can sleep.'

'I'll wait outside until you're in bed.'

For heaven's sake! After the door had closed, Cory slipped out of her clothes without opening her eyes and moving the least she could. She didn't bother trying to find her nightie, which was folded up in the bedside cabinet, sliding under the thin summer duvet with a sigh of relief.

A few minutes later she heard the door open and then a deep voice at the side of her said, 'There's a drink of water beside you if you need it.'

'Thank you.' Go, just go.

'Are you warm enough? You were cold earlier.'

In actual fact she was still cold; migraines always seemed to make her feel that way. There was a quick debate in her aching mind as to whether she should admit to it or just send him home. 'There's a hot-water bottle in the bottom of the chest of drawers,' she said, her eyes closed. 'It's got a Winnie-the-Pooh cover on it.'

A moment's pause, and then he said, 'I've got it.'

In no time at all he was back. When she heard the door open Cory slid an arm from under the covers. 'Thanks.' She was feeling worse if anything. She'd had special medication prescribed for her at university, but since the migraines had waned and then disappeared altogether once she was working she hadn't renewed the prescription. She wished now that she had. Her aunt's aspirin wasn't even touching the pain.

'Anything else I can do?'

'No. No, thanks,' she added, knowing she'd been too abrupt.

'I'll leave you to get some sleep then.'

She was aware of his lips brushing her brow and then the door closed again.

She lay completely still because the slightest movement jarred her head unbearably, and after a few moments she heard the front door close. He had gone. Tense muscles relaxed. If she was sick again at least she could do it without an audience!

Then she berated herself for being so nasty when Nick had tried to be so nice. But she'd lied to him when she'd said the nausea only happened once; often it was two or three times, and throwing her heart up in front of him wasn't exactly the picture she wanted him to carry home in his mind.

The aspirin must have worked to a small degree because she dozed for a while. She had no idea of how long she'd been in bed when she suddenly knew she had to get to the bathroom again.

Throwing back the duvet, she struggled to her feet but after making the mistake of opening her eyes once she

didn't try it again, feeling her way out of the room. She
reached the bathroom without mishap, only to find the
waves of nausea receding. She felt behind her gingerly for
the bath and sat on the edge of it as she tried to decide if
she dared go back to bed.

'What are you doing?'

The shock of Nick's voice brought her eyes open and a
thousand daggers pierced her brain. She was as naked as
the day she was born and here he was spying on her! 'What
am *I* doing?' she croaked furiously, grabbing a bath towel
and pulling it round her. 'What are you doing? I heard you
go ages ago.' She glared at him, colour flooding her face.

'I went to a local pharmacy for something a bit better
than aspirin,' he said with magnificent aplomb. But then he
wasn't the one with no clothes on. 'I was going to give
you a couple of pills when you woke up.'

'You've been here all the time?' She shut her eyes again,
partly because the pain was too intense to keep them open,
but mainly because she didn't dare look at him a moment
longer. He had seen her stark naked and not in a nice romantic way either. No—his first sight of her totally in the
buff had had to be when she was feeling like death and no
doubt looking it too. And he had added insult to injury by
switching on the light as he'd walked in the bathroom. Her
cellulite would have been positively screaming at him.

'I've been kipping in the chair in the sitting room.'

That would have been fine if he had stayed there.

'Come on, get back to bed and I'll fix you a hot drink
so you can have a couple of these pills,' Nick said comfortably, as though he hadn't just put her through her worst
moment ever. It didn't help that in the brief glare she'd
indulged in she'd noticed a dark stubble on his chin which
made him look ten times more sexy than usual, if that were
possible. That and the open-necked shirt and rumpled hair.

'It's three in the morning, so if you have a couple now you might start feeling better towards lunchtime when you wake up. I'm assured these knock you out like a light.'

She wished he'd woken her up when he'd fetched them then. Before she'd decided to lumber blindly about the flat in her birthday suit.

Cory pulled the towel tighter round her and stood shakily to her feet, allowing him to lead her back to the bedroom because it was easier than arguing. Once she was in bed she lay listening to the sounds from the kitchen, but the pain was so bad again her embarrassment had vanished. Nevertheless, she made sure the duvet was wrapped round her like a second skin when she sat up to take the warm milk and pills Nick brought.

'Thank you.' It was reluctant, which wasn't very nice, she admitted to herself.

'My pleasure. Drink it all up.'

He didn't actually add, like a good girl, but he might as well have, Cory thought bitterly, swallowing the pills and finishing the milk before she snuggled under the covers again. Obviously the sight of her in the altogether hadn't stirred him in the least.

'You really can go now,' she said as she heard him walk towards the door. 'You said yourself I'll sleep till lunchtime.'

He didn't answer, merely closing the door gently behind him, which was somehow more aggravating than any argument.

The next time Cory opened her eyes there was a chink of bright sunlight stealing through where the curtains had parted a little, but she found it didn't cause her to wince any more. She felt incredibly tired and somewhat fragile, but the piercing pain was a thing of the past, just a normal sort of headache remaining.

She moved her eyes carefully to the little alarm clock on her bedside cabinet, experience warning her that any sudden movements could remind the pain to return. One o'clock. *One o'clock?* She really had slept till lunchtime, she thought in amazement. But there was no doubt she felt better, much better.

Was Nick still here? Now she could open her eyes without fear of the laser, she slowly sat up and reached into the cabinet for her nightie. Once it was on she felt better, even though she was dying for a bath.

He wouldn't still be here, surely? But then she would never have dreamt he would remain last night. Her cheeks flamed as she remembered the incident in the bathroom. But it *had* been nice for him to be so concerned. She hadn't expected that somehow.

She swung her legs out of bed and rose to her feet. Her head thudded a little, otherwise she didn't feel too bad. She found her bathrobe and fluffy mules, brushing her hair through at her dressing table and groaning at the sight of her white face. She looked awful, just awful. Still, she'd probably looked even worse last night. It wasn't particularly cheering.

She visited the bathroom, cleaning her face with the lotion she used and then brushing her teeth vigorously. She compromised on the bath by having a quick sluice down, promising herself a long hot soak later. Five minutes later and she was in the kitchen, looking at Nick who was busy cooking bacon. He had looked round and smiled at her entrance before saying, 'I was going to bring you a tray but now you're here we'll eat at the breakfast bar.'

Her tiny kitchen was nothing like his and the breakfast bar was barely big enough for two but Cory didn't point this out, merely sitting with a little plop on one of the stools. She was still more shaky than she'd thought.

'How are you feeling?'

The blue eyes briefly met hers again and Cory found she had to lick dry lips before she could reply. His five o'clock shadow was definitely designer stubble now. If she'd thought he looked sexy before it was nothing to now. 'Lots better,' she managed huskily. 'And thanks for staying and the pills and everything.'

'All part of Nick Morgan's bedside manner service.' He cracked eggs expertly into a bowl and began to whisk them. 'Help yourself to orange juice and pour me one, would you,' he said over his shoulder.

She stared at his back. Considering what she had decided the night before in her Aunt Joan's bathroom, Nick making himself so at home here was not a good idea. It was too cosy, too…poignant. It spoke of things which could never be and she was going to find it hard enough as it was once he had gone from her life. But she couldn't very well tell him to leave, not when he'd spent the night on her sofa because he'd been concerned about her. It wouldn't have been so bad if she'd had a guest room for him to sleep in, but her second bedroom was her study and clutter room.

He turned round, putting a rack of toast on the breakfast bar before skimming her mouth with his lips. He had returned to the bacon before she could react. 'Peppermint,' he said thoughtfully.

'What?'

'Your taste this morning. Peppermint.'

'I brushed my teeth,' she said unnecessarily. 'Nick, we have to talk. What we were discussing last night at my aunt's, I don't know…' She faltered, not knowing how to go on.

The muscles across his back had tensed but his voice

sounded perfectly normal when he said, 'Not before break-fast. I'm starving and I can't talk on an empty stomach. Besides which, you need something inside you so you can have another of those pills. Just one this time, though.'

'I'm not hungry.'

He turned with two plates, putting one in front of her and sitting beside her as he began to eat. 'Eat, Cory,' he said softly. 'We can talk another time. Don't worry.'

She risked a glance at him and then wished she hadn't. She wanted him. She wanted him so much. She reached for a slice of toast and put a little of the scrambled egg from her plate on it. Mechanically she began to eat. Another time he had said. So she didn't have to say good-bye today. It was worth the migraine.

CHAPTER SIX

CORY sat staring at the case file spread out on the desk in front of her but her mind was miles away. Should she have taken the bull by the horns and said something before Nick had left yesterday? She'd had plenty of opportunities because he had stayed most of the afternoon.

She wriggled in her seat. But it had been so *nice*, she wailed silently. Special. She had lain with her head in his lap on the sofa and he had stroked her hair as they had talked a little and dozed quite a lot. He had been tender and gentle and relaxed; it had been one of the few times when she'd been with him and had not been assailed by a hundred and one different emotions, all of them disturbing.

He had looked after her, she thought with a feeling which was half pain and half pleasure. He hadn't thought of his own needs at all; he'd just been wrapped up in caring about her.

The phone on her desk rang and she picked it up automatically, still thinking of Nick. 'Miss James. How can I help you?'

'I can think of a good few ways and all of them X-rated.'

'Nick?' She could hear the warmth in her voice herself and tried to moderate her tone as she continued, 'What are you doing ringing at ten in the morning?'

'Enquiring how my favourite girl is,' he said smokily.

Cory shut her eyes. She could just picture him sitting at his desk, black hair slicked back and face freshly shaven. He would probably have discarded his suit jacket as soon as he'd got to the office and for certain his tie would be hanging loose. He hated the constriction of a tie. She took a deep breath. 'More or less back to normal, except for feeling ridiculously tired, but a few early nights will fix that.'

She wondered if he'd picked up on the subtle hint that she wouldn't be seeing him that night. She had known as she'd waved him goodbye the evening before—after a kiss which had set her toes tingling, never mind the rest of her— that she had to cool things down rapidly. It was time to take a big step backwards and maybe if she did that he would do the same. If this relationship could just wane naturally it would all be for the best. Wouldn't it?

'Sure,' he agreed lazily. 'Best thing.'

She frowned at the phone. He wasn't supposed to say that. And then she caught the pique, angry with herself for her inconsistency. She wanted him to bow out of her life gracefully on the one hand but on the other she wanted him to fight tooth and nail to see her every moment. She was a bundle of contradictions and she was driving herself mad, never mind Nick. Nevertheless her voice was cool when she said, 'That's what I thought.'

'The other reason I'm ringing is to say I'm out of town for a few days from this afternoon. I've been putting off a trip to Germany for some time but certain reasons make it imperative I go this week.'

'Oh, right.' Suddenly the sunshine streaming through her office window was less bright, the sky less blue. 'I…I hope it goes well,' she said in a small voice.

'It will.' He sounded positive and forceful and clearly couldn't care less that for the first time since they'd been seeing each other they would be spending some time apart.

Cory was suddenly furiously angry with him. She knew it was unreasonable but she couldn't help herself. She also knew she had to wait a moment before she spoke because the last thing she wanted was for him to pick up on how she was feeling.

'Cory? Are you still there?'

'Yes, sorry. Someone was handing me something,' she lied quickly.

'I'd better not keep you any longer. Look after yourself and don't work too hard. I'll ring you.'

'Yes, all right. Bye.'

'Bye, sweetheart.'

The receiver went click at the other end but Cory stared at the phone in her hand for some seconds before slowly returning it to its stand. Sweetheart. She couldn't remember him calling her that before and his voice had been different when he'd said it—warm, soft, as though he'd really meant it.

Stop it. She was thinking again and she thought too much. She had decided action was the only answer to this incredible tangle she'd got herself in, and action spelt distance in this case. She just hadn't expected it would be Nick who would do this distancing. But that was fine, just fine. It *was*. It had to be.

Nick rang just as she was getting into bed that night. 'Cory? It's Nick. I haven't got long but I wondered how you're feeling. Headache still under control?'

She sat on the edge of the bed stupidly, her mouth opening and shutting, her heart pounding at the sound of his voice. She hadn't expected him to call. 'I feel fine,' she said at last, her voice thankfully steadier than she felt. And then, as a burst of laughter came down the line, she added, 'Where are you?'

'Out to dinner with some people. Sorry, it's a bit noisy but it's the first chance I've had to call.'

'You shouldn't have bothered.' That sounded awful.

'You've plenty to think about without worrying about me,' she qualified quickly.

'Perhaps I want to worry about you,' he said softly, or as softly as the background din would allow. 'Anyway, it's unlikely I'll be able to call the next day or so and I wanted to tell you to keep the weekend free. I'm taking you somewhere.'

'Taking me somewhere?' She was so surprised she forgot to tell him she couldn't possibly go. New regime and all that.

'Somewhere nice.'

'Somewhere nice?'

'Cory, you're repeating everything I say,' he said patiently. 'Look, I've got to go.' The noise swelled even more. 'I'll see you Friday evening. Pack a bag.'

'Nick—'

'Dream of me.' It was husky and deep and she felt the impact trickle over her nerves like warm honey. 'Only of me.'

'Nick—'

'Because I'll be dreaming of you, especially now I've seen exactly what I'm missing.'

Cory blinked. She had been quite impressed that he hadn't mentioned her *faux pas* yesterday; she might have known he couldn't keep it up. 'That was below the belt,' she said with what she hoped was haughty displeasure.

'Below the belt, above the belt, I saw it all.'

She knew he was grinning. She could hear it in his voice.

'And very nice it was too. More than nice...'

She heard someone call his name. A female voice.

'Look, I have to go,' he said quickly. 'They've brought us out for dinner after a meeting that went on for hours; they're so hospitable.'

Yes, well, they would be, wouldn't they? Cory thought

waspishly. She bet 'they', whoever they were—and there was certainly one woman among them, at least—didn't get many British visitors who looked like Nick Morgan. 'Nick, about this weekend—'

'Bye, sweetheart.' The line went dead.

Two sweethearts. Cory stared at the carpet. Two sweethearts *and* a weekend away somewhere. This was definitely the lead up to the big seduction scene. Maybe he had even planned the trip to Germany to make her miss him and be more receptive when he got back?

And then she immediately dismissed the thought, telling herself not to be so cynical. Nick wasn't into mind games the way William had been. If she didn't believe that she wouldn't still be with him.

But she couldn't go away somewhere, to a lush hotel or whatever, and then tell him that far from sleeping with him she actually was going to end their affair. She would have to talk to him as soon as he got back to England; failing that, when he arrived to pick her up on Friday evening. That was if he didn't call her again in the meantime.

She rubbed her hand across her face to wipe away the tears seeping down her cheeks. How would she bear not seeing him again? How was she actually going to say goodbye? But far better to do it now than in a few months, a year, even a couple of years, by which time she would be unable to exist without him. This was self-preservation at its rawest.

By Friday evening Cory was a nervous wreck. In spite of knowing she was determined to go nowhere with Nick Morgan, she found herself packing an overnight case—just…in case. Which really made her a candidate for the funny farm, she told herself wearily, glancing at her watch. Six o'clock. Nick knew she usually arrived home from work about five-thirty. He could be here any minute. Her stomach turned over and she had to sit down suddenly. Of course he might be much later.

She had missed him more than she would ever have believed possible this last week. She had dreamt about him when she was asleep and when she was awake and had made some elementary mistakes at work which had caused her to start checking her paperwork over and over again. She hadn't felt the slightest bit hungry all week—that was the only bonus in days and nights of misery because she had lost three pounds.

She had phoned his office at lunchtime but his secretary had told her he was arriving back in England some time in the afternoon, and no, she didn't have any idea if Mr Morgan was coming into the office or going straight home. Cory didn't know if she altogether believed this, but the secretary would say exactly what Nick had told her to say, that was for sure. He must have known she was less than enthusiastic about going away for the weekend by the tone of her voice when he'd called her from Germany. That being the case, his astute and intelligent mind would know he had far more chance of persuading her if he stood before her in the flesh than by speaking to her on the telephone.

And he was absolutely right. Cory groaned out loud. In all her dreams she'd woken filled with a raging hunger for his embrace, an intense longing to feel his arms round her and his mouth on hers. He was just too good at everything he did, that was the trouble, and his lovemaking was top of the list.

When the door buzzer went a moment later Cory jumped so much she nearly fell off her chair. Telling herself she had to be the most feeble woman in the world, she walked over to the intercom in the hall. 'Hallo?' she said flatly as the butterflies in her stomach did the tango.

'It's me.' Just two words but they had the ability to make her start trembling.

'Hi.' She breathed deeply, willing herself to calm down. 'Come on up,' she said, leaning with one hand against the front door as her legs threatened to give out.

She was still standing in exactly the same position when he knocked on the front door moments later.

You can do this, she told herself firmly, ignoring the racing of her heart. Just be cool and calm. No tears, no hysterics, no big scene. The 'we can still be friends' scenario, even though you know you can't.

She opened the door. Nick was leaning against the stanchion, an enormous bunch of flowers in his hand. He wasn't smiling; in fact, his expression was one she hadn't seen before, almost brooding. The next moment she was in his arms, the flowers tossed carelessly on to the carpet.

He covered her lips with his in a kiss of such explosive desire that the world stopped, or Cory's world at least. He'd kissed her hungrily before, passionately, until her legs had become weak and her mind befuddled, but nothing—nothing like this.

Her arms had wrapped round his waist and she pressed against him, wanting to absorb his heat and his strength, needing to fuse their bodies together. Curves melted against hard angular planes, rock-hard thighs against soft feminine places until neither of them could have said where one body began and the other finished.

Nick pulled his mouth away for a millisecond to fill his lungs, but then his mouth returned to hers as though he couldn't bear even a moment of separation. His tongue touched hers, probing, urging her to respond, and she gave herself up to the wonder of pure sensation.

He had moved one hand to her head to hold her in place, one leg slid between hers to bring his lower body in alignment with her hips as he moved her against the hall wall, pinning her against him. The action both eased and increased the rocketing sensations shooting to every part of her body and she caught her breath at the sharp pleasure.

'Hell, I've missed you.' He lifted his head slightly so he could look into her face. 'You've no idea...'

She had. Oh, she had.

'I've dreamed of doing this every hour of every damn night.' He bent his head again to tease one corner of her mouth with his tongue, before kissing her cheek, her jawline, then forging a burning trail to her ear.

'Say you've missed me,' he murmured, his breath in her ear making her shiver with delicious anticipation. 'Say it.'

'I've missed you.' She arched against him, her body saying it too. 'So much.'

He shifted her in his arms, his hands running over her soft curves and cupping the fullness of her breasts through the soft fabric of her top. She gasped against him and he smiled, a slow, masculine smile that made her toes curl. 'You feel great,' he said very softly. 'You taste great. You are great.'

'So are you.'

He chuckled into her mouth. 'Not good enough. You've got to give your own accolades, not steal mine.'

Her eyes were heavy, her mouth swollen with his kisses. 'You're amazing,' she murmured dazedly. 'Will that do?'

'For starters.' He shifted her in his arms but then, instead of continuing to make love to her, he reached down and picked up the discarded flowers. 'Put them in water before we go,' he said quietly.

If she hadn't noticed his hand shaking slightly she would have thought he was totally in control, despite the hard ridge of his arousal which had been forged against her only seconds before. The sight was comforting; she was trembling so much she knew he must see it. She took the flowers without saying anything, walking with them into the kitchen where she buried her hot face in the fragrant free-sias and soft white roses. She drank in their perfume, not thinking, not allowing any thought to come into her mind. Then she filled a vase with cool water and put the bouquet in it just as it was. She would arrange them properly when she came back.

Because she was going. She was going to have this one weekend if nothing else, she told herself, still a little dazed and numbed by the powerful emotions which had been re-leased between them. It was probably the most stupid thing she would ever do in her life, a guarantee of emotional suicide at some point in the future, but suddenly she didn't care. He was here, here with her, and for the moment that was enough.

'Where are we going?'

They had been travelling for some miles before Cory asked the question, her voice low and husky. She was still registering the sensations which had taken her over at the flat—the way their bodies had fitted together, the pleasure given and received, the wonder of the world of passion and need and hot desire he'd taken her into.

'Guess.' He gave her a quick smile. 'You know about this place but you've never been there.'

'That applies to more parts of Britain than it should.' She wrinkled her nose. 'I'm not exactly a seasoned trav-eller.' She kept her eyes on him as she spoke although his gaze had returned to the road through the windscreen. He looked hard and dangerous and too sexy by far. He was dressed more casually than usual and she knew he must have gone to the flat before coming to see her. His formal suits or tailored trousers had been replaced by well-washed black jeans, tight across the hips, and his open-necked black denim shirt emphasised his flagrant masculinity more than any silk shirt could have done.

Suddenly it dawned on her. 'We're going to your home,' she said. 'The house in Barnstaple.'

'Quite right.' He reached for her hand and brought it up to his mouth, kissing her knuckles. 'I thought it was about time you saw where I live.'

'You live in your flat.'

'No.' The blue eyes flashed her way for a moment. 'I only occupy that. There's a difference.'

She stared at the dark profile. He'd shaved recently; there was a tiny nick on his chin where he'd cut himself. The rush of feeling this produced was scary.

'Besides which I thought you might like to meet a few of the family,' he continued casually.

'Your family?'

'I was thinking of the one next door,' he said with gentle sarcasm. 'Of course my family. Why? Does that bother you? They're really quite normal.'

Cory didn't know what to say. She wanted to ask if he usually took his girlfriends home to meet his family but she didn't dare. Of course it was highly likely that he did, she warned herself quickly when her treacherous heart did a few cartwheels.

'It seemed a good time with my mother's birthday being on Sunday,' he added.

'Your mother's *birthday*?' She sat bolt upright in her seat, all the nice floaty sensations that had stayed with her from the episode at the flat gone in a moment. 'It's your mother's birthday and you didn't tell me? I haven't got a card or a gift for her.'

'She won't be expecting one,' he said with typical male denseness regarding the niceties of such occasions.

'Of course she will.' Cory was horrified. 'Have you bought her anything?'

'I'll get something tomorrow,' he said calmly, his voice stating there was no need to get in a panic. 'When I've asked her what she wants. Something for the house, maybe.'

Men! Cory shut her eyes for a moment. 'A nice new vacuum cleaner, perhaps?'

He seemed quite oblivious to the sarcasm.

'Nick, your mother is a woman, in case you haven't noticed,' Cory said evenly. 'Do you ever get her something for herself? Chocolates? Flowers? A book? Clothes?'

'Clothes?' She could have suggested something obscene, such was his scandalised expression. 'Of course not. I have bought her chocolates and flowers before, though.'

There was some hope for him then. 'And I bet she loved them, didn't she?'

'My mother always loves anything I buy her.' There was a definite note of hurt in his voice now. 'It's the thought that counts, isn't it?'

So they said. And it must have been a man who coined the phrase. 'We'll shop tomorrow,' she said, 'for something for you to give her and something for me. What's she like? Describe her to me.'

'My mother?' His mouth twisted in a wry smile. 'She's quite a woman.'

She would have to be to have a son like you.

'She and Dad had the sort of relationship where they'd be hammer and tongs one minute and then falling into each other's arms the next—two strong minds, you know?'

She nodded.

'But us kids never doubted how much they loved each other or us. Dad was the more staid, upright one, very conventional—typical lawyer, I guess.'

'Your father was a lawyer?' Somehow she'd assumed he would have been a businessman like Nick.

'A damn good one.' There was a wealth of affection and pride in his voice and it touched her deeply. 'Mum...' He smiled again. 'Mum is one on her own. A true original. Nonconformist, feisty, stout-hearted. Dad used to say she was sent to keep him humble.'

Cory smiled but she thought Nick's mother sounded a bit scary. 'Does she work?'

'She was involved in animal welfare when Dad first met her but while we were young she did the housewife bit and thoroughly enjoyed it. Once my youngest sister was at school she started doing one of her great loves—painting— and also went back to the animal welfare thing, but in a smaller way. She does voluntary work at a local sanctuary. On the painting side—' he paused briefly while he executed a driving manoeuvre Cory was sure was illegal and which caused several other motorists to make use of their horns '—she's done very well. She sells all over the country now.'

Cory was feeling more nervous by the minute at meeting this Superwoman. 'What about your sisters?' she asked a little weakly, feeling she didn't really want to hear the answer.

'Rosie's thirty years old, married her childhood sweetheart at eighteen and has two kids, Robert who's ten and Caroline who's eight. She's utterly content being a wife and mother and is in nature a carbon copy of our father. Jenny's twenty-eight, travelled the world with a backpack from eighteen to twenty-three, married an artist who has his own pottery business and had twin girls four months after the wedding.' He raised a laconic eyebrow. 'That was a couple of years after Dad died, which is just as well as he'd have blown a gasket.'

Cory giggled. 'The twins are about three, then?'

'A few weeks before Christmas.'

'You sound like quite a family.'

His mouth curved upwards in a crooked smile. 'When Jenny and Rod called the girls Peach and Pears, Mum thought the names were terrific and Rosie and her husband were horrified. There isn't a more devoted aunt and uncle than Rosie and Geoff though. Sums us up, really.'

'What about you?' she asked interestedly. 'What did you think about the names?'

'Jenny had survived what proved to be a traumatic birth when she haemorrhaged and we nearly lost her and the twins were well and healthy. They could have called them Noddy and Big Ears as far as I was concerned.'

Male logic. Cory smiled. 'I like Peach and Pears,' she said very definitely. 'I don't see why people are locked into tradition about names. Flower names are considered perfectly proper so why not fruit or anything else for that matter?'

'Do I detect a smidgen of bohemian coming through? Is it possible that in the future you might be considering artichoke or cabbage, or even New York if the unfortunate infant was conceived away from home?'

Her smile faded. She didn't reply for a moment and then she said flatly, 'I don't intend to have children.'

'Perhaps all for the best if cabbage is a possibility.'

His voice was light and easy and he was smiling, but the warm intimacy in the car was gone and they both knew it. Cory felt a moment of deep regret that she had broken the mood.

The nifty little sports car fairly ate up the hundred and seventy miles or so to Barnstaple once they were out of London, but it was still almost dark when they neared the coast.

For some reason Cory was feeling an illogical sense of panic at the thought of seeing Nick's house. She couldn't actually have said why. It wasn't so much that this was the weekend she would finally take the plunge and go to bed with him, more that this house—his *home*—would reveal more about him than the flat ever could. And what if she didn't like what it revealed? Certainly the flat, beautiful as it undoubtedly was, didn't do a thing for her. But then he had said he didn't *live* in the flat, merely occupied it.

The morning star was high in a sky which was turning from mauve washed with midnight-blue to deep velvet-black when the car finally turned off the wide, pleasant avenue they'd been travelling along for a minute or so. A smaller road, almost a lane, took them past several houses set in beautifully manicured grounds. After several hundred metres there were no buildings at all, just the high stone wall one side and to their left rolling fields in which the round white bodies of sheep stood out in the evening shadows. Then the stone wall curved round in front of them, forming the end of the lane, and after drawing to a halt Nick opened the wrought iron gates set in the wall by remote control.

This was going to be some property! Even before they drove on to the long gravelled drive winding between established flower beds and mature trees, Cory was preparing herself for her first sight of Nick's home. And then there it was in front of her. A large mellow-stoned thatched building flanked either side by magnificent horse chestnut trees, its leaded windows on the ground floor lit by lights within the house.

'Good,' Nick murmured at the side of her. 'Rosie's remembered to leave the lights on. She always comes in and stocks up the fridge when she knows I'm coming home,' he added as they drew up in front of the huge stone steps leading to the front door.

'Nick…' For a moment Cory was devoid of speech. 'This is beautiful, just beautiful.'

He smiled at her in the shadows, his blue eyes glittering. 'I fell in love with the place the first time I ever saw it,' he admitted softly. 'It dates from 1703, although bits have been added here and there. Come in and have a look.'

The minute Cory stepped into the wide gracious hall she knew the inside of the house was going to match the outside. Warm-toned oak floorboards stretched into every room on the ground floor, their richness interspersed with big rugs. The huge sitting room, which overlooked the grounds at the back of the house, had big squashy sofas, one wall lined with books, low coffee tables and an enormous fireplace with a pile of logs in one corner ready for burning. The dining room, big breakfast room, Nick's study and the farmhouse-style kitchen complete with Aga were all beautifully decorated but with a cosy feel to them which ran throughout the house.

By the downstairs cloakroom off the hall an open tread wooden staircase led to four generous-sized double bedrooms, all with *en suite* bathrooms, and a gigantic master bedroom. This room caused Cory to take a sharp breath when she first entered it. It wasn't the walk-in dressing room, which would have swallowed her sitting room at home, or even the *en suite* bathroom, which was more luxurious than the one in Nick's flat that was the trouble. It was the bed. It was unlike any bed Cory had ever seen. In fact, it was more of an ocean of billowy space than anything else.

That he had been expecting her discomfiture was obvious in the amused tilt to his mouth when he said, 'You might have guessed I had the bed made specially. I'm a big boy; I like a lot of room.'

'You've certainly got that,' she squeaked weakly, wondering how many of his women he had shared it with.

It was set in front of huge windows, which had the same outlook as the sitting room below, the three carpeted steps which led to it the same length as the bed. The duvet and numerous pillows and cushions were various shades of coffee and taupe and this colour scheme was reflected through the whole suite. The bed was sensual and outrageous and sinful; it dominated the whole room and declared without any apology that pleasure was its chief aim.

Cory had to clear her dry throat before she could say, 'The...grounds look very nice from what I can see in the dark.' Nick had switched some outside lights on before he had begun to show her round the house, and now an area stretching some distance from the building was revealed.

'Oh, it is nice, Cory,' he said seriously.

Too seriously. She glanced at him sharply. He was laughing at her. She knew it, but she also knew she needed at least two glasses of a good wine before she could relax enough to contemplate that bed with any confidence or, more to the point, the man who slept in it.

She could just imagine the model type beauties who normally graced its languorous folds, she thought miserably. Suddenly all her imperfections had ballooned to giant size—particularly the vastness of her bottom and the dimples she could see at the tops of her legs when she looked hard enough. And Nick would be looking.

'What's outside, exactly?' she asked with what she hoped was cool dignity.

'Exactly?'

He grinned that fascinatingly sexy grin and Cory upped the wine to three glasses.

'Let's see. Covered swimming pool and sauna which can be reached via a door off the kitchen as well as from outside. I'll show you when we go downstairs. Plus a tennis court and croquet lawn, an orchard and a walled garden, which is very old-fashioned but quite cute. And lawns and trees and bushes, of course.'

'Wow.' Her eyes had widened. 'Quite a bit of land then.'

'A bit, but manageable. I have a gardener come in once a week for a few hours.'

She nodded. Another world really. Her parents hadn't been badly off and she had certainly never wanted for anything materially, but this sort of wealth was a thing apart. Of course she'd known his little empire was successful— he'd told her early on in their relationship that he'd been in the right place doing the right thing at the right time— but confronted with this beautiful house the reality of how rich he must be hit her for the first time.

She became aware that he was studying her face, the amusement gone from his eyes. 'Relax, Cory,' he said softly. 'This is Nick, not William, remember? You're allowed to leave this room without being ravished if that's what you want. I wanted you to see my home, that's all.'

That was only half true and she knew it. He wouldn't be human if he wasn't hoping for more from this weekend and he had been patient, allowing her time. They couldn't go on as they had been doing; their relationship either had to end or go on to the next stage.

And then suddenly he took her hand, his voice quite normal when he said, 'Come and look at the pool and then we'll see about some supper and a glass of wine. It's a gorgeous night, how about we take it outside?'

'That'd be nice.' Her relief was overwhelming. No doubt girlfriends in the past had just gaily stripped off and jumped into bed without a thought in their pretty heads except how to please him and how he could please them—young, care-free, eager beauties who were self-assured and modern without any hang-ups. She envied them. How she envied them.

The pool complex was gorgeous but they didn't tarry there. The very capable Rosie had packed Nick's fridge with everything needed for a romantic supper for two, and within a short while they were sitting outside at the patio table, which was spread with all sorts of delicious delicacies. Nick had apparently asked his sister to put a bottle of champagne on ice, and after pouring two glasses he handed her one, saying, 'To us.'

It was a perfect summer's night. Stars overhead, the stone beneath their feet still retaining the day's heat and the garden bathed in a moonlit silence which was magical. The air was rich with the perfume of scented stock and fragrant night lilies which were in pots all around the patio, a faint breeze carrying the delicious scents on its meanderings.

Cory breathed very deeply and took a sip of the ice-cold champagne that tasted faintly of strawberries. 'I wonder that you can bear to leave here for the city.'

'So do I tonight.' His voice was husky and his blue eyes held hers in the glow from the candles he had lit before switching off the outside lights. The house behind them and the grounds stretching in front had all been relegated to the shadows of the night; it was as if they were the only two people in the world in their flickering circle of light.

Cory shivered suddenly but the chill was from within, not without. She wished he had been an ordinary sort of man—one who did a nine to five job, who was perhaps a little overweight, who maybe had smelly feet. There might have been a chance he wouldn't grow tired of her then. But that was silly—he wouldn't be Nick and she wouldn't love him if he was any different. She'd ignored the caution light even when it had turned from amber to red, flashing its danger sign in great big letters. *Don't let him into your heart and your life.* Yes, she'd ignored it. She only had herself to blame.

But she wasn't going to think of all that now. She gave a mental shrug. There was tonight, this entrancing garden and Nick. Her blood heated, singing along her veins. If this one weekend was all she had, then it would be enough.

CHAPTER SEVEN

WHEN they had finished the dessert Rosie had brought—a wickedly frothy concoction of raspberries, dark chocolate and meringue topped with lashings of thick cream—Nick disappeared into the house with the dishes and empty champagne bottle to make the coffee. He refused to let Cory help, kissing her very thoroughly before he left until she felt she was drowning in the taste and feel of him.

She sat in the balmy quiet of the scented garden, wrapped in a sensual glow that didn't fade before he returned. As he placed the coffee tray on the table she wrapped her arms round his neck, pulling his mouth to hers. 'I've missed you,' she said throatily, half smiling.

'I'll have to leave you more often.' He kissed her again before he straightened, adding, 'Drink your coffee. It's one of my specials.'

'Specials?' She picked up her cup, running her tongue dreamily over the creamy foam. It tasted wonderful. 'I didn't know coffee could taste like this. What's in it?'

'I told you, it's one of my specials. I've quite a range,' he said lazily. 'This one's got spices and whipped cream and a coffee liqueur a friend of mine from Brazil brings me when he's in this neck of the woods.' He sat down in his seat again, stretching out his long legs, his body relaxed and at ease.

Cory glanced at him from under her eyelashes as she sipped at the fragrant drink. The black denim added to the aura of masculinity and he made her legs weak. Tonight he would take her into that enormous bed. The morning could take care of itself.

They talked of inconsequentials as they sat there, the flickering candles slowly burning down and the star-studded sky above. When Nick at last rose to his feet, pulling her up with him, Cory felt a brief moment of panic.

She wasn't experienced like his other women. She didn't know any little tricks or moves to keep a man interested in bed. She just had herself to offer and suddenly that didn't seem nearly good enough.

As he put his arm round her she shivered. 'Cold?' He pulled her tighter into the warm protection of his body. His hands began caressing her, their touch as light as down and unthreatening. Slowly she relaxed, her head falling back against his shoulder, her eyes drowsy with desire as they met his. He lowered his head, nipping and teasing at her lips between planting little kisses on her chin, her nose, her closed eyelids. When his mouth finally took hers, his tongue thrusting deep into the warm moisture within, it was a kind of consummation, a woman accepting the powerful thrust of a man inside her body and Cory moaned softly.

He led her into the house still wrapped in his arms and they walked slowly up the stairs, each step punctuated with more caresses and soft murmurings. When they reached the landing Cory didn't realise for a moment where he was leading her. Then, as he opened the bedroom door and she stared into the pretty room beyond, her eyes opened wide. 'But I thought...'

'What did you think, sweetheart?' he asked softly.

She stared at him, so taken aback she didn't know what to say.

'That coming away with me for the weekend was some sort of sexual blackmail?' he continued silkily. 'I told you before, I'm not William.'

'I know.' Her voice was barely a whisper and his face gentled.

'No, you don't, not yet. Make no mistake, Cory, I want you. I want you so much I walk the floor some nights when cold showers don't do the trick. But you're not ready yet. Did you think the reason I told you I loved you before I went to Germany was to set you up for this weekend?'

Now he had voiced it she realised it had been at the back of her mind all the time. But she shook her head. 'No, of course not.'

'I've told you before, you don't lie too well,' he said with a faint little smile. His eyes searched her face. 'I want your trust as much as your body, Cory. Can you believe that? And this minefield of your past has to be cleared before that can come about. The only way I know to make it happen is to show you who I am. If you don't trust me then anything we have will be built on shifting sand; the first strong wind that comes against it will send the whole pack of cards tumbling.'

Cory's throat was locked and she couldn't utter a sound. She had never felt more confused in her life.

'You're bound up by fear; you know that, don't you?'

'Fear?' It unlocked her voice. 'I'm not afraid.'

'Yes, you are. I thought it was of me to begin with but the more I've got to know you, I see it's not that. It's Cory James who frightens Cory James.'

She took a little step away from him. 'I don't know what you're talking about,' she said, backing into the bedroom.

'You're frightened that the person you are isn't good enough or worthy enough or whatever it is.' A note of anger was in his voice for the first time. 'It's a legacy from your parents and it's rubbish, Cory. You know there's a part of me that could almost feel sorry for William if the guy hadn't been such an out-and-out jerk.'

'*What?*' Now she was angry. It put adrenalin where it was needed and burnt up the feeling of a few moments before which had had her wanting to cry. 'Why?' she snapped.

'Because you were waiting for him to let you down, weren't you? All along. And when it finally happened it confirmed you had been right. He had followed the pattern. You damn near led him into it.'

'I did not!' Her face was flushed; she glared at him, her hands clenched at her sides. 'How dare you say that?'

'Think about it,' he ground out. 'You picked a low-life who was programmed to treat you badly because that's the way he treats any woman in his life. It's a kind of victim mentality.'

'*Victim?*' It was fortunate that Nick had brought her to his home rather than a hotel because Cory's shout of sheer outrage would have woken every guest in the place.

She didn't have to think about what to do next. Her hand shot out with such speed it surprised them both, but Nick more so. Her last sight of him he was nimbly springing backwards as she slammed the door shut with enough force to have broken his nose but for his quick reflexes.

How dared he? How *dared* he say those things to her? She called him every name under the sun under her breath. And to think she had been going to sleep with him tonight; she must have been stark staring mad. She would never forgive him for this, never. If it wasn't the middle of the night she'd be straight out of here to find the nearest railway station.

She stood, breathing hard, glaring at the door, half-expecting he might knock or at least try to speak to her but there was no sound at all. He wasn't going to apologise. As the realisation swept in she became even madder.

She swung round to survey the bedroom. Her overnight

case was on a chair by the bed so he had obviously intended that she would sleep alone even when they had arrived at the house. Her cheeks began to burn but the anger was mixed with humiliation now. He must be having a good laugh at her expense.

She marched across to the *en suite* bathroom, opening the door and surveying the expanse of cream and gold which echoed the colour scheme in the bedroom. She was glad to see there was a nice big bath because if ever she needed a long soak rather than a shower it was now.

Thirty minutes and a refill of hot water later, Cory's rage was beginning to be replaced by self-pity. Half an hour after that she began to ask herself if there was a grain— just a grain—of truth in Nick's accusations. At three o'clock in the morning, after two hours in the bath and with her skin resembling the texture of a shrivelled pinky-white peach, she finally admitted to herself that he did have a point.

But she hated him. She rubbed herself vigorously with a towel before wrapping herself in an enormous bath sheet and padding through to the bedroom, her hair dripping wet. He needn't have been so offensive, and as for saying he felt sorry for William!

He hadn't actually said he felt sorry for William, a little voice in her head reminded her fairly.

As good as, she answered it militantly. Oh, yes, as good as. Well, that was fine, just fine. At least she knew where she stood now. He obviously thought she was off the wall and as weird as a cuckoo; if only he'd made that clear before he invited her down here it would have saved them both a lot of trouble. And she didn't give a damn what he thought anyway.

The tears came about four o'clock, but after a good howl she fell fast asleep and slept through until a knock on the bedroom door woke her. She opened her eyes to a room filled with sunlight and lay for a second of absolute confusion as to where she was. Then she remembered. As another knock sounded she scrambled up in bed, glancing around frantically as though a hole would open up in front of her.

Calm, girl, calm. As her thudding heart threatened to jump into her throat, she forced herself to take a deep breath. He was a rat and she loathed him. That being the case, she would treat him with utter contempt this morning and be on her way out of his life as soon as she was up and dressed. She refused to reflect on what she must look like with no make-up, eyes swollen from the tears of the night before and her hair—which had dried itself—one giant tangle.

'Come in,' she called tightly, adjusting the duvet under her armpits with her arms lying across her lap and her hands clasped.

'Good morning.'

He had the nerve to smile at her, she noticed, as he came into the room carrying a tray holding a cup of tea and a small plate of biscuits. She also noticed that he was wearing a black cotton robe and matching pyjama bottoms, and his hair was damp from the shower. He hadn't shaved either. He was devastating. 'Good morning,' she answered grimly.

'Sleep well?'

Swine. 'Perfectly well, thank you.'

'Breakfast will be another half an hour or so, but I thought you might like a cup of tea. I assume it is tea you drink in the mornings rather than coffee?'

She stared at him. She always had at least two cups of tea before she could begin to function in the mornings but she was blowed if she was going to admit that he was right about anything today. She shrugged, taking the tray as he came to stand close to the bed before nodding her thanks. 'Not really,' she lied coolly. 'Either are fine.'

'Funny, I'd got you down as a tea girl.'

He'd got her down as a lot of things as he'd made only too plain the night before. After taking the tray she refused to look at him, keeping her eyes on the teacup. 'Really?' she said, putting a wealth of disinterest into the one word.

'You're mad at me.'

Dignified contempt, remember, she warned herself silently. She raised flinty brown eyes. 'Why would I be mad at you?' she asked coldly.

'I don't know, unless it's because I've made you face up to a few things.'

The sheer arrogance took her breath away, that and the way the tight black curls on his broad chest—visible through the loosely tied robe—gleamed like oiled silk in the sunshine spilling into the room. 'Hardly,' she said stiffly.

'You sulk beautifully.'

The thread of amusement in his voice was reflected in the quirk to his mouth and Cory was sorely tempted to throw the tea over him. She just couldn't bear to spoil the exquisite broderie anglaise cover on the quilt, though—that and the inch-thick cream carpet. Besides, she told herself, she'd decided on cool disdain and that was what she was sticking to. 'Where is the nearest railway station?'

'Why?' he asked calmly.

'Isn't it obvious?'

'Not to me.'

'Well, I wouldn't dream of bothering you to run me back to London when you've only just got here,' she said with heavy sarcasm.

'Good.' He had been standing looking down at her but now he sat on the bed. Cory's senses went into hyperdrive.

'But you aren't going anywhere other than to do some shopping with me today, so cut out the childish tantrums and finish your tea.' He leant forward as he spoke, depositing a firm but swift kiss on her lips before standing again and walking to the door. 'I mean it, Cory,' he said evenly, all amusement gone from his face and voice. 'You're spending the weekend here. You're meeting my family. End of discussion.'

She glared at him, hot colour burning her cheeks. How could he make her feel like a recalcitrant child when he had been the one who was way out of line? 'You can't keep me here by force,' she said tightly.

'No, I can't, nor would I want to.' He stood with his hand on the door handle, eyeing her with the piercing blue gaze which seemed to look right into her soul. 'I was being cruel to be kind last night, can't you see that?'

'I thought that was the excuse people normally trot out when they are caught mistreating someone or something.'

'Then you thought wrong, in this case at least. I spoke as I did because I care, Cory. Think about it.' He opened the door and exited the room before she could answer.

She sat, trying to ignore the dull ache in the region of her heart that his last words had produced. She wanted to stay mad at him. She *needed* to stay mad at him. By his own admission he had been cruel last night. How could he say he had been like that because he cared about her?

Her parents had never had sufficient interest in her to tell her any home truths, either as a child or a young woman.

The thought hit her with the force of a ten ton truck. She couldn't remember a time when they had actually focused on her or got angry with her like Nick had done last night, she thought sickly. They had spoken sharply many times, usually to send her back to her room if she had left it for too long or if she was asking for their attention over something or other. But to take time to think about her or worry about her or even wonder why she behaved the way she did just hadn't been in their scheme of things. They hadn't cared enough.

She sat quite still, the tea cooling in her hand. Nick had said he cared. He'd also said he loved her before he had gone to Germany. But what exactly did he mean by that? How much? How much did he care?

With the tea now quite cold she got out of bed and carried the cup into the bathroom, tipping the contents down the basin. When she raised her head she caught sight of herself in the mirror and immediately any other thought was swept away by the sight of the scarecrow looking back at her. Her face was pale except for her eyes, which were faintly puffy and red-rimmed. Her hair gave the impression she had been pulled through a hedge backwards.

Whatever had he thought? She groaned. Even in her worst days at home she looked better than this.

Once she had showered and put a little light moisturising cream on her face she applied some careful make-up, which improved things no end. She brushed the tangles out of her hair with the help of a leave-in conditioner, looping it into a high ponytail once it was smooth and wavy.

Better. She inspected the result as she sprayed a dab of perfume on each wrist and the back of her neck. Much better.

Once in the bedroom she dressed swiftly in a sleeveless linen shift, sliding her feet into a pair of flip-flops and fixing small silver studs in her ears. She glanced into the full-length mirror by the bed. Casual, cool, without appearing to have taken too much effort. As a damage control exercise it would have to do. She took a deep breath. Now to face Nick downstairs.

He was sitting in the breakfast room, its French doors open to the fresh scents from the garden and a row of covered dishes at one end of the big pine table. He looked up as she entered, throwing the newspaper he had been reading to one side as he rose to his feet.

He had waited to eat with her. She felt a glow of pleasure out of proportion to the act of courtesy.

'Hi,' he said, very quietly. 'How about we start over again?'

She stared at him. 'Yes, please.'

'Does that mean shopping and lunch later?'

She nodded.

'Good.' He grinned at her. 'I thought I was going to have a fight on my hands. I wouldn't have let you go, you know.'

She wanted to ask him why but she dared not. 'I still don't think you put it very well,' she said, determined to have her say before they put it behind them. 'And that remark about William was uncalled for. But overall...' She hesitated.

'Overall?'

'There was some truth in what you said.'

'Thank you.' The grin widened. 'That was hellishly hard to say, wasn't it?' he added sympathetically.

She didn't trust the sympathy any more than she trusted her weakness where his charm was concerned. 'Hellishly,' she agreed crisply, determined not to smile. 'Could I have some juice, please?'

'Help yourself.' He waved a hand at the table. Besides the covered dishes there was a mountain of toast, preserves, a jug of freshly squeezed orange juice and a pot of coffee.

Cory suddenly found she was ravenously hungry and more happy than she would have dreamt herself being an hour ago. She filled her plate with scrambled egg, bacon,

mushrooms and crisp hash browns, sitting down and beginning to eat with gusto.

Nick had done the same although his plate was filled
with twice as much. She had just put a particularly succu-
lent mushroom in her mouth when she sensed his gaze on
her. She looked up. 'What?'

'I'm so glad you're not one of those women who push
the food round on their plate for half an hour, or sit with
a nice juicy something on their fork while they talk on and
on,' he said appreciatively. 'The times I've wanted to lean
across and tell a woman to get on with her food.'

She frowned at him. 'How rude.'

He chuckled softly. 'I've never claimed that patience is
one of my virtues.'

And yet he had been terribly patient with her in the last
couple of months since they'd met.

Her face must have betrayed something because now it
was Nick who said interestedly, 'What?'

'Nothing.' She wasn't about to give him any accolades
after last night. He might be right in essence about William
but she hadn't quite forgiven him for pointing it out so
brutally. And she definitely didn't agree with the victim bit.

It was a new experience for Cory to go shopping with a
man and she found she loved it, probably because the man
in question was Nick, she admitted to herself ruefully. It
was nice shopping too—not trundling around a busy su-
permarket or anything like that.

She purchased a fairly generic card for Nick's mother,
and then watched with concealed amazement as he scanned
all the different verses in the 'son to mother' cards on dis-
play. The one he eventually chose was surprisingly senti-
mental.

'She places a lot of importance on the words,' he said

somewhat defensively as they walked out of the shop. 'She always maintains the best ones were the cards we made ourselves when we were children. She's kept them all.'

Cory smiled and said something appropriate but his words had hurt her. She would have given anything for a mother like that.

She hadn't let Nick call his mother and ask her what she wanted that morning before they had left the house. 'She would love a surprise,' she'd told him firmly. 'All women do. And not anything practical. OK?'

And so here they were after just an hour, with Nick having bought an elegant Louis XVI-style chair and matching footstool made from kiln-cured beech, the fabric being cream linen with velvet leaf appliqué. Nick had assured her his mother would go ape for the chair and had paid a hefty charge for it to be immediately delivered. 'She's been looking for something like this for her bedroom for years,' he said with a great deal of satisfaction. 'She'll love it. Trust me.'

Cory's comfort was rooted in the fact that the chair and footstool would at least be a surprise.

She had opted for a pair of exquisitely fashioned silver earrings from a small jeweller's in the heart of Barnstaple. The tear-shaped drops were inset with onyx, the semi-precious agate used to dramatic effect against the precious metal.

Nick had approved of her choice with reservations, as she had with his.

Later that afternoon he dropped the bombshell that they were in fact expected to attend a family party in honour of his mother's sixtieth birthday. They were sitting enjoying a relaxing cup of coffee in an enchanting little patisserie at the time. 'Nothing formal,' he assured her when her countenance changed dramatically. 'Just a casual get-together this evening.'

'How casual?' she demanded, her brain immediately doing an inventory of the clothes she had brought with her.

'Nibbles, drinks, dancing.'

'Where?'

'At a local hotel.'

She wondered if the owners of the little patisserie had ever had a man strangled in their establishment.

The next hour was spent in a frantic search which yielded a black and silver asymmetric dress in silk linen, which went perfectly with the black ankle-strap sandals she had thrown into her case at the last moment.

They arrived back at the house at six-thirty and were due at the hotel for drinks with the immediate family before the other guests started arriving at seven-forty-five.

Cory tore up to her room like a mad thing, clutching the bag with the dress in it. She had less than an hour to transform herself into an elegant creature of the kind usually seen on Nick's arm.

She was back downstairs at seven-fifteen; made-up, coiffured and feeling a lot more confident in the black and silver silk linen than she would have done in the smart-casual dress she had brought with her for evenings.

She found she had to take a deep breath at the sight of Nick. He had dressed up in black dinner jacket and tie. He had been sitting waiting for her in the hall, one leg crossed over the other knee, and now he stood up at her approach. The blue eyes stroked over her in a way that made her hot.

'You look good enough to eat,' he said softly. 'But the taxi's arrived so I'll have to restrain myself.'

'Pity.' She smiled brightly. 'But we don't want to keep your family waiting, do we?'

She'd decided she would emulate his other women tonight. She was going to be sophisticated and vivacious, carefree. The dress had cost more than she would have ideally liked, but when she'd slipped it on earlier a certain devil-may-care attitude had come with it. She was tired of being herself; she wanted to be someone else for a change. Nick had accused her of being childish and it had rankled. Tonight she'd show him she was very much a woman.

'Remembered the present?' he asked her as he opened the front door.

'It's in my handbag.' The jeweller's had wrapped the earrings beautifully.

'Then we're set.' He smiled at her, taking her arm as they walked to the waiting taxi. Just for a moment she saw them as an outsider would see them. A wealthy and handsome man with a well-dressed woman on his arm. Elegant, glittering, the sort of couple who had everything. Funny how different things could be from what they appeared on the surface.

Once in the taxi Nick pulled her close, his arm round her shoulders. It was a nice way to travel, more than nice. She could detect the hint of primitive musky male beneath the clean, sharp aftershave he was wearing. It was a heady combination.

He must have appreciated her perfume because after a few minutes he said huskily, 'What's that scent you've got on tonight?'

It had been an expensive Christmas present from Aunt Joan and she didn't wear it often. 'Why?' She turned her head to look up at him. 'Don't you like it?'

He took her hand and placed it on the hard ridge in his trousers. 'Need I say more?'

'*Nick.*' He had shocked her and it showed. So much for the cool sophistication.

He chuckled and she knew he'd got the result he wanted.

'You're beautiful, Cory, inside and out,' he said softly. 'And the wonder of it is you really don't think so.'

'I'm not beautiful.'

'You are.' He kissed her. 'Like a rare orchid or a precious stone.' Another kiss. 'Or a shooting star that leaves a trail of silver.' His lips were warm and erotic. 'Or a cactus flower that only blooms every few years.'

She wrinkled her nose. 'Cactus are spiky.'

'I know.' His smile was gentle. 'But the flower is worth waiting for.' This time he took her lips in a soul-stealing kiss that made her weak at the knees.

When she had regained her breath, she said, 'Do you think your mother will like me, Nick?'

She hadn't meant to ask but it had bothered her all day. She had been wondering how many women had been introduced to his mother and whether any of them had been particular favourites with Mrs Morgan.

'No, she won't like you,' he said softly. 'She'll love you, like I do. They all will.'

She stared at him, her eyes wide.

He held her gaze. 'Do you believe that?' he said quietly as the taxi sped on through the late August evening. 'That I love you?'

She hadn't expected this now, not here. But Nick was the sort of guy who was full of surprises. Unable to speak for the violent pounding of her heart, she settled for a slight nod of the head.

'That's an improvement on the last time I said it.' He ducked his head to nibble at her earlobe. 'It's still not the response I'm looking for,' he said after a moment or two when she had to bite her tongue to stop herself moaning out loud, 'but it's an improvement.'

Just then the taxi bumped over a hole in the road and they were thrown even closer together, his arms tightening as her rounded curves pressed against his hardness. 'Do you think we'd be missed if I told him just to keep driving all night?' Nick murmured in her ear.

'Possibly.' But she was game if he was.

When the taxi drew up outside the sort of hotel that featured in glossy magazines, Cory's nerves jangled. Meeting his family *en masse* suddenly seemed like torture. She found herself clutching Nick's arm so hard he actually winced, at which point she let go. 'Sorry.'

'The others'll be in the lounge bar,' Nick said quietly once he'd paid the driver and they were standing outside. He tucked her hand through his arm. 'Now relax, OK?'

'I don't think I can,' she said shortly.

'It's no big deal.' He turned her round to face him with his hands on her shoulders. 'They'll love you, Cory. I know they will. But even if they didn't it wouldn't make any difference to us. I'm a big boy now, in case you haven't noticed. I don't have to ask for my family's approval on my girlfriends.'

She knew that but it didn't help because she so wanted them to like her. She lifted her chin and now it was she who slipped her arm through his. 'Come on,' she said evenly. 'We don't want to be late.'

When they walked into the lounge bar it was immediately obvious where the Morgan contingent was by the calls and waves that met them. 'This is Cory,' Nick said as they approached the corner where three tables had been drawn together.

She smiled at the blur of faces and everyone smiled back, then Nick was kissing his mother and sisters and after a moment or two there were introductions all round. Nick's mother wasn't at all as Cory had expected from his description. Instead of a somewhat fierce Amazon, a small, dainty and very beautiful woman smiled at her, kissing her on both cheeks before she said, 'Cory, how lovely to meet you. I'm so glad you could come.'

His sisters were equally warm in their welcome, Jenny proving to be a carbon copy of her mother whereas Rosie was big, stolid and hearty. So was her husband, a tall blond man with red cheeks, whereas Jenny's husband was slim to the point of boyishness with floppy shoulder-length hair and an easy grin.

The only person who didn't seem pleased to see Cory was a voluptuous redhead whom Nick's mother introduced as, 'Margaret, my god-daughter. Margaret's a lecturer at Leeds University and doing awfully well.'

Margaret's handshake was cool, her smile more so, but Cory noticed it hotted up a good few degrees when the redhead turned her lovely green eyes on Nick. 'Nick, darling.' The voice was upper-class and well modulated. And warm, very warm. 'Why haven't you called me lately, you naughty boy?'

Cory kept her smile in place with some effort. So that was how things were? This woman liked Nick. In fact, from the way she was devouring him with her eyes, Margaret liked Nick very much. She watched as Nick gave the other woman a perfunctory kiss on the cheek, much as he had done with his sisters, before moving on to shake the hands of his brothers-in-law.

'Darling, my beautiful chair and stool. I love them, they're perfect. And what a surprise. I couldn't believe it when Hannigan's van drew up and the man said it was a special delivery for me.' Nick's mother reached up and kissed him, her eyes glowing. It was clear she was thrilled.

Nick's face was full of love as he looked down at the diminutive woman in front of him. 'I'm glad you like them,' he said softly. 'But the surprise part was Cory's idea. I was going to ring up and ask what you wanted.'

'Happy birthday, Mrs Morgan.' Cory handed Nick's mother the small package from her handbag along with her card.

'Oh, call me Catherine,' Nick's mother said, touching Cory's arm in a quick, friendly gesture before taking the gift. 'May I open it now?'

'Please do.' Cory would rather she'd waited until there wasn't quite such an audience, but as the tiny box revealed its contents Nick's mother was delighted. 'They are exactly what I would have chosen,' she said warmly. 'How did you know? I've always been a bit of a gypsy,' she added in an undertone to Cory, 'and I just love dangly earrings. These go perfectly with what I'm wearing tonight.' So saying, she whipped out her present earrings and substituted the ones Cory had bought, moving her head slightly so that the teardrops swayed against the line of her jaw.

'Looks like we both chose well,' Nick whispered in Cory's ear a moment or two later. He had just ordered champagne cocktails all round.

She nodded. 'Your mother's lovely,' she said quietly. 'You're very lucky, Nick.'

'I know it.' He was looking into her eyes as he spoke and his voice was deep and soft.

The next moment Cory became aware of Margaret at their side. All the others had sat down again and now, as Rosie reached out and touched Cory's arm, asking her if she had been to Barnstaple before in an obvious effort to be friendly, Cory had no choice but to smile at Nick's sister and take the seat Rosie patted beside her.

All the time she was talking to Nick's sister she was vitally aware of the two people at the perimeter of her vision, however. Nick appeared to be his usual relaxed self from the odd glance she managed to throw his way, but Margaret seemed to be talking very intensely, her voice low but her body language suggesting it wasn't a normal conversation.

After a few minutes Nick took the seat on Cory's other side, putting his arm round her shoulders as he leant across to join in the discussion she and Rosie were having about the advantages and disadvantages of being near the coast. Cory welcomed his nearness; she had felt a bit odd talking to Rosie with Nick and Margaret so intent on each other.

By the time they had transferred to the big function room where the party was being held and the other guests had started arriving, Cory knew she liked Nick's family very much. His two sisters were as different as Nick had indicated, as were their husbands, but underlying their dissimilarity Cory sensed a bond that was unbreakable.

Catherine Morgan was very much the matriarch of the family but in the nicest possible way, and her respect for her children and their individuality was obvious. That each child adored their mother was also obvious, and as Cory noticed the easy relationship Catherine had with both her sons-in-law she reflected that Nick's mother was a wise as well as loving mother.

The nibbles Nick had spoken of turned out to be a full-scale buffet at ten o'clock, and as Nick had paid for an open bar all night everyone was enjoying themselves to the full—some a little too much. But everyone was pleasant and happy and the band was excellent, and as far as Cory was concerned it was wonderful to be in Nick's arms again on the dance floor.

She had danced with Nick's brothers-in-law and he had danced with his sisters a couple of times, as well as his mother, but Cory noticed he hadn't asked Margaret to dance. Margaret had stuck to their table like glue, slipping into a seat on the other side of Nick when folk had first begun to occupy the tables scattered around the dance floor.

It was around one o'clock in the morning, when Nick was having a last dance with his mother—Catherine having stated a minute or so before that she had called a taxi to take her home but that the rest of them must continue enjoying themselves—that Cory found herself in a conversation about Margaret with Jenny. Nick's sister was standing at the buffet table idly chewing on a stick of celery when Cory joined her, with her eyes fixed on her husband and Margaret, together on the dance floor.

'Look at her,' Jenny said in an undertone, with the candidness that was typical of her. 'She can't resist trying to bewitch every man who crosses her path. Poor Rod looks scared to death. He's not used to dancing with a praying mantis. And it was me who told him to ask her to dance, with her not having a partner. He'll never forgive me.'

Cory couldn't help laughing. Jenny's husband did have a hunted expression on his face. 'Why didn't she bring someone? I can't imagine she'd have any problem in finding a date.'

'Because of Nick, of course.' And then Jenny clapped her hand over her mouth. 'Sorry, that was incredibly tactless.'

Cory's stomach had done a flip but she managed to keep her voice casual. 'No, it's all right. I'd gathered she likes him.'

'Likes him?' Jenny eyed her grimly. 'She's like a leech at any family do but with her parents being great friends of ours Margaret's always been around. Funnily enough, her mum and dad are really nice. You'd like them. They're away in the Caribbean at the moment, though.'

Cory nodded. She wasn't interested in Margaret's parents.

'Look, let me explain something.' Jenny took her arm, leading her to a quiet corner. 'Nick would kill me if he knew I was talking like this so don't let on, but I think it's better you should know. So you don't get the wrong idea.'

Cory kept her face bland even as her heart sank like a stone. She wasn't going to like this, whatever it was.

'Margaret's always had a thing for Nick, right from when we were all kids together. She's Rosie's age and with our parents all being friends she was always at our house, supposedly to play with Rosie and me but in reality to traipse after Nick and his pals. When Nick married Joanna, well…' Jenny paused as if not knowing how to go on.

'Margaret didn't like it?' Cory put in.

'That's putting it mildly. She was nearly eighteen when we heard Nick and Joanna had done one of these sudden registry office things but even at that age she thought she was the cat's whiskers. I honestly don't think it had occurred to her that Nick might not want her. Then Joanna was killed.' Jenny shook her head. 'It was a bad time.'

'I can imagine.' His shock and grief must have been terrible.

'Nick came home for a while, more to decide where his life went from that point than anything else, but Margaret was never off the doorstep. It must have driven him mad. It certainly drove him away,' she added bitterly.

'That's a shame.' He would have needed his family desperately.

'Then, all of a sudden, she was off to university and seeing this boy and that. I mean she *really* put it around,' Jenny said darkly. 'She got a First, went on to greater and greater things, got married, then divorced, and we all thought she was over Nick. Then a couple of years ago she and Nick had a bit of a fling over the summer. Just a no strings attached type of affair. She actually told me herself that's what they had decided. She'd got this terrific job at the university—I mean she's brilliant, quite brilliant—and

Nick's always made it plain where he stands on commitment.'

Jenny stopped abruptly, looking at her anxiously.

'It's all right.' Cory forced a smile. 'He's made it plain to me too.'

'But since then she's been...odd. She's trying to get him back, I'd swear it.' Jenny sighed deeply. 'So just watch out for her, that's all I'd say. I wouldn't trust her an inch.'

'You don't like her.' Cory stated the obvious.

'Loathe her.' Jenny shrugged. 'But she's Mum's goddaughter and Mum likes her. Feels sorry for her a bit, I think. The thing is, if someone thinks your child is the bee's knees you can't help liking them, I suppose.'

Great. Had Nick's mother always hoped he'd marry Margaret so everything in the garden would be hunky-dory? If so, she'd view all his girlfriends as obstacles.

As Jenny bounced away to rescue Rod as the dance ended, Cory's mouth drooped. She watched Jenny join Margaret and Rod, who were walking off the dance floor with Nick and his mother, and Catherine had one arm through Margaret's and the other through Nick's. It looked cosy. Natural. Happy families.

Nick's eyes were searching the room and then as he saw her he lifted his hand and waved, leaving the others. She couldn't see the expression on Catherine's face as she was obscured by a young couple walking by, but Margaret looked straight at her, her eyes deadly.

Then Nick reached her, taking her in his arms as he murmured, 'I've missed you. We've been apart for five whole minutes. Mum's going now; come and say goodbye till tomorrow.' All the family were going to Catherine's for Sunday lunch.

For the next hour or so until the party finally broke up Cory said and did all the right things. She laughed and joked with the others, danced with Nick and avoided Margaret's lethal green gaze.

On the way home she pleaded exhaustion when Nick asked her why she was so quiet, and, refusing a nightcap— which would be much more than a mere liqueur coffee if Nick's smouldering gaze was anything to go by—went straight up to her room. And then regretted bitterly that she hadn't stayed with him.

She sat down on the bed with a little sigh, feeling as flat as a pancake. Which was crazy when she thought about it because nothing had changed. Nick had said he loved her. Fine. He had probably loved all his women, or the long-term ones at least. She *knew* that, so what difference did it make if he and Margaret had slept together a couple of summers ago and Catherine Morgan would like her god-daughter as a daughter-in-law too? He wasn't going to marry Margaret any more than he was going to marry her, so feeling upset and jealous and put-out was plain stupid.

It didn't matter if she was here on sufferance as far as Nick's mother was concerned. It didn't matter, that Margaret was far more a part of Nick's life long-term than she was. It didn't even matter that Margaret was going to be at Nick's mother's tomorrow where she'd no doubt be a limpet attached to his side.

None of it mattered. She burst into tears.

One good cry, a scrub of her face and a brush of her teeth later, Cory climbed into bed, the exhaustion she'd spoken of real. It had been a long day after just a couple of hours' sleep the night before. She was asleep as soon as her head touched the pillow.

CHAPTER EIGHT

A GOOD night's sleep worked wonders. Cory awoke wide awake and alert—not a normal occurrence for her—at nine the next morning, and she was in a different frame of mind entirely. Climbing out of bed, she walked across and drew the curtains and immediately bright sunlight flooded the room. It was another gorgeous day. Flinging the windows wide, she leaned on the sill and breathed in the scent of the climbing roses beneath her, their heady, rich scent a wonderful start to the day.

She wasn't going to let all this about Margaret get her down. She turned from the window, staring across the room. She *wished* she'd stayed downstairs with Nick last night but there you were, she hadn't. She groaned softly. No use crying over spilt milk. But today was another day. And she was here in his home and Margaret wasn't.

That was when the idea came to her. Nick had brought her tea in bed yesterday morning. OK, why didn't she return the compliment? And once she was in his bedroom...

She hurried into the bathroom, had a quick shower and then brushed her hair until it shone with health. After putting a coat of mascara on her eyelashes and a dab of perfume behind each ear, she cleaned her teeth. She hoped he wasn't up yet but they had been terribly late last night and it *was* a Sunday. He was probably still dead to the world.

Her nightie was a floaty negligée type which consisted of very little, another gift from her aunt a couple of Christmases ago. She knew it was one of those horribly expensive designer things but she had never worn it until this weekend. She considered herself critically in the mirror. What the transparent film did to her body would have been enough to make her love her aunt for life if she didn't already.

Cory sped down to the kitchen with wings on her heels, hoping Nick wasn't already there. He wasn't. She made a pot of tea in record time, setting a tray with two cups and saucers, sugar bowl and milk jug, and adding a little plate of biscuits for good luck.

She had actually got to the door of the master suite when she stopped abruptly. What was she doing? Was this a good idea? She was going against all reason here. Hadn't she told herself that if she once got totally involved with Nick it would be emotional suicide? What would she do when he left her? And one day he *would* leave her.

It was too late anyway. She answered herself with total honesty. She loved him. Utterly and absolutely. She wanted to be with him for as long as he would stay with her. It was as simple as that. It probably was the biggest mistake she would ever make in the overall scheme of things because she didn't know how she'd survive when she had to do without him, but that was the future. This was the present. And the present was all that mattered.

She opened the door to the bedroom very quietly, tiptoeing into the room and over to the enormous bed. It was empty. She stared at it, utterly taken aback. And then she heard whistling in the bathroom.

Putting the tray on a small table which was half covered with Formula One magazines, she walked over to the bathroom door, which was open a chink. She didn't think about what she was doing, she was just drawn there by an invisible cord.

Nick had obviously just stepped out of the shower and was drying himself down. He was nude. Cory's heart did the sort of giant leap for mankind the astronauts had spoken of.

Six foot plus of lithe, tanned muscle and he was breathtaking, that was the only word for it. The wide shoulders and broad chest were strong and sinewy, his lean hips and hard buttocks unashamedly male. The hair on his chest narrowed to a thin line bisecting his flat stomach before forming a thick black mass wherein his masculinity stood out in startling white. He was a perfect specimen of manhood. A male in his prime.

Cory had stopped breathing. She was just looking. And looking. And then it dawned on her just what she was doing. Invading his privacy, spying on him, behaving like the worst sort of peeping Tom. What would she say if the tables were turned and she had caught him sneaking up on her?

She swallowed, panic rising up hot and strong as shame overwhelmed her. Stepping backwards, she stood trembling and weak, her cheeks flaming but her senses still stirred by the magnificence of him. She had to get out of here. She would die, die on the spot if he found her ogling him like a lovesick adolescent.

As the whistling stopped it prompted her to the door like a silent rocket and she shot along to her room with her feet hardly touching the ground. Once inside, she flung off the nightie, pulling on the first clothes which came to hand, which happened to be jeans and a T-shirt. Stopping just long enough to pull her hair back into a ponytail, she hightailed it back down to the kitchen.

She had to be cooking breakfast when he came down. He had to think she had just put the tray in his room and come down here. And then she groaned. Two cups. Two cups of tea on the tray. Well, she'd just say she thought he was probably thirsty in the mornings. She shut her eyes tightly. He would think she was mad but that was better than thinking she was some sort of sex-starved nymphomaniac!

She got busy cracking eggs into a bowl and putting bacon and tomatoes under the grill with a couple of minute steaks she found in the fridge. The toaster doing its job, the coffee pot bubbling and fresh juice on the table, she relaxed for a second. Her hands were shaking.

What had she been doing creeping about up there? That wasn't her; she wasn't like that. But that was the trouble, she didn't know what she was like any more. Since she had met Nick her whole world had been turned upside down and she didn't know if she was coming or going most of the time. And thinking she could seduce him with a flimsy nightie and a tray of tea! She groaned softly.

'What's the matter; are you feeling ill?'

She swung round, knocking a pile of toast on the floor in the process. 'You made me jump,' she said breathlessly, trying to see him as he was—clothed in jeans and a shirt—rather than stark naked.

'Sorry, but you made a sound as though—'

'I was thinking about a case I'm working on.' She was lying more and more since she had met him too. She wasn't even getting any better at it if the look on his face and his raised eyebrows were anything to go by.

'Right.' Thankfully he didn't pursue the matter. 'Do you want me to do the scrambled eggs because the bacon's burning,' he said helpfully.

'Damn!' She couldn't even cook a simple breakfast now.

Between them they salvaged the bacon and cooked the eggs, and once they were sitting down Nick reached across and took her hand. 'The tea in bed was nice of you,' he said softly, 'but I was hoping the other cup had been intended for you.'

Cory forced a brittle smile. 'Of course it wasn't.' She knew her cheeks were fiery and hoped he'd put it down to the mad scramble with the food. 'I wanted to cook breakfast for you. You did it yesterday, remember.'

'So I did.'

'And I thought we wouldn't want to eat too late if we're going to your mother's for half-twelve.'

'Quite right.'

'So that's why I got going on it.'

'Yes, you don't have to spell it out. I've got the idea.'

She was gabbling. She crammed a piece of bacon into her mouth to stop herself saying anything more. It was hot, burning hot. She spat it out as her tongue caught fire and then said, 'I'm sorry, that's awful, but it was hot and—'

'Cory, have I missed something this morning?'

'What?' She stared at him, horrified. 'What do you mean?'

'You're like a cat on a hot tin roof.'

She relaxed slightly. 'It's sleeping in a strange bed,' she improvised hurriedly. 'I never sleep well in a strange bed and then when I wake up I tend to be a bit…jumpy.'

'Oh, I see.' He took a bite of steak and chewed it slowly, swallowing before he said lazily, 'I thought it was because you saw me in the shower.'

She stared at him, utterly bereft of words.

'I didn't mind,' he added calmly, reaching for a slice of toast and spooning some scrambled egg on it. 'In fact, I think I rather enjoyed it. Of course I'd have preferred you to stay, but by the time I came into the bedroom, you'd vanished.'

He knew. She prayed for the ground to open up and swallow her, or at least for her to be able to think of something to say rather than sitting staring at him with her mouth open like a stranded fish.

Eventually she managed to croak, 'It's not what you think.'

'I don't think anything.' The blue eyes held hers and they were glittering with suppressed laughter. 'This is an excellent steak, by the way. You've cooked it just how I like it.'

Blow the steak. Cory swallowed. 'I thought I'd give you a cup of tea in bed as you'd brought me one yesterday,' she said stiffly. 'As I was leaving, the door was ajar and I just happened…'

'Ah, I thought that might be the case.'

She stared at him. 'You didn't actually see me then?'

'Of course not.' He smiled serenely. 'Do you think I wouldn't have pulled you in there with me if I'd seen you?'

'Then how…?'

'The two cups of tea were something of a give-away.' He was positively smug. 'I just put two and two together.'

Cory called him a name which nice, well brought up ladies didn't say—not often, anyway.

'What's the matter?' He looked at her with an injured expression. 'It was me in the nude, not you.'

'I know that,' she said through gritted teeth.

'So why are you the one complaining?'

'I'm not complaining,' she said icily, her voice in stark contrast to her cheeks, which felt as though they were melting. 'I just don't like being tricked, that's all.'

'But if I hadn't got it out of you you'd have been suffering a guilty conscience all day,' he said with insufferable complacency. 'This way we've cleared the air and everything is back to normal.' He took another bite of toast as he added, 'Did you like what you saw, by the way?'

She glared at him.

'OK, end of discussion.' He smiled, reaching out and stroking one hot cheek as he said, 'I love it that you can blush. It's a lost art, you know. Most women are so hard-boiled these days nothing bothers them.'

Most women wouldn't run like startled rabbits if they saw a man in the nude. She took a swallow of juice because it was easier than having to think of something to say.

'You were a great hit last night, by the way.' He smiled over the top of his coffee cup. 'My sisters are crazy about you.'

'What about your mother?' It was out before she could stop it, and something in the tone of her voice must have alerted him that all was not well.

'Mum, too.' The piercing blue gaze homed in on her.

'Good.' It was flat.

'Really.' He reached out and took her hand, lifting it to his lips in one of the little endearing gestures she found so special. 'My mother likes you; you must have sensed that?'

She nodded. 'I like her too.'

'What is it?' His voice was quiet, all amusement gone. 'Was something said I don't know about?'

She couldn't let Jenny down. She forced a smile to her face. 'Don't mind me,' she said quickly. 'Just feeling insecure being the new kid on the block, I guess.'

'You did great,' he said, but it was automatic. 'Cory, you'd tell me if something was wrong? If someone's upset you?'

How could she say that she knew she wasn't really wanted, by his mother at least? That Margaret was destined for him? It would look as though she was criticising Catherine for a start and she wouldn't want to do that. She didn't blame Nick's mother for wanting the best for her son, and Margaret, with her stunning looks and super-intelligent brain, had more to offer him than she did. 'Nothing's wrong.' She had to defuse the tension. She reached out and touched his hand. 'I had a lovely time last night and it was great to meet everyone.'

I love you so much. I don't want to be a ship that passed in the night in a few years.

She couldn't bear to look at him a moment more without saying something they would both regret. She took her hand away and reached for her coffee cup instead, beginning to make light conversation about his sisters and their children. Nick fell in with her mood, making her laugh about some of the antics of the twins in particular.

After breakfast Nick loaded the dishwasher while she wiped the table in the breakfast room, and then they went for a stroll in the grounds to work off the breakfast.

The tennis court and croquet lawn were immaculate, and the trees in the small orchard were gently basking in the summer sunshine, but it was when Nick led her to the walled garden that Cory became absolutely enchanted. It was set behind the orchard and clearly very old, as the ancient walls, mellow and sun-soaked, proclaimed. Nick opened the gate which creaked as they stepped inside, and Cory just stood and stared for a moment.

The stone walls were brilliant in places with trailing bougainvillea—purple, red and white flowers all jostling for space beside the green and red of ivy. There were a host of scents in the air, a winding path meandering past squares and circles of raised flower beds, old trees, borders of hollyhocks and marigolds and secluded bowers with seats surrounded by climbing roses.

'Nick.' She clutched his arm as she spoke but continued to feast on the scene in front of her. 'This is just the most perfect place in the world.'

He smiled, his voice soft as he said, 'It was neglected and overgrown when I bought the house but still beautiful. My gardener is an old guy with a great deal of soul. He gentled it all back to perfect health by letting the garden tell him what it wanted.'

She looked at him, surprised. He'd sounded almost poetic.

He caught the look and his smile widened, crinkling the corners of his eyes. 'That's what he says, anyway. Come in and have a wander.'

The path led them past sweet-smelling shrubs and bushes specially chosen for their individual fragrances, an old statue of a little girl with a puppy at her heels cast in bronze and weathered by time, the odd fountain or two tinkling their music into ancient stone troughs and crumbling stone bird tables all bearing traces of seeds. 'Albert loves the birds,' Nick said as he caught her glancing at the seed.

'I like Albert.'

The garden was an oasis of peace and tranquillity, the only sound the gentle hum of bees going about their business and the twittering of birds in the branches of some of the old trees above their heads. There were butterflies galore, bright and colourful as they fluttered from one sweet-smelling bush to another. It was a magical place. A place she'd remember all of her life.

'I would spend hours just sitting if I owned anything like this,' Cory said dreamily. 'Sitting and watching and letting the garden talk to me.'

'You'd get on like a house on fire with Albert,' Nick said wryly. 'He takes it as a personal insult that I don't inhabit the place twenty-four hours a day.'

'How often *do* you come in here when you're home?'

He shrugged. 'Not often.' And as she continued to look at him. 'Rarely.'

'What a waste.'

'Albert enjoys it.' They had reached the gate again, having done a full circle, and now they stood together looking at the colour in front of them. 'And I've been tied up with the business the last umpteen years. There hasn't been any time for sitting and watching and listening to gardens talk.'

'That's a shame,' she said quietly. 'To work as hard as you do just for other people to enjoy what you have.'

He stared at her, clearly taken aback. 'It won't always be that way.'

'When won't it be?' she asked directly. 'When is enough, enough?' And then she turned away. 'But it's nothing to do with me, of course.'

For a moment he didn't speak. Then he said, 'You of all people should understand how it's been for me. You said yourself your career is your life and that you don't want anything else to come before it.'

Had she said that? She supposed she had. But since she had got to know this complex individual at the side of her it had gone out of the window. There were other things which could work alongside her career, things which ultimately could come before it. In a strange sort of way she felt she had been sleeping the last twenty-five years and had only just woken up.

She kept her eyes on an exquisite red admiral butterfly sipping nectar from a profusion of scarlet and white lily-type flowers. 'Perhaps I was wrong,' she said softly. Perhaps she had been wrong about a lot of things. She might appear to be sure about where she was going and what she wanted from life, but the self-analysing she'd done since getting involved with Nick had shown her she was still the shy, nervous little girl who had been programmed never to reach out to anyone. And she didn't want to live the rest of her life like that. Whatever happened between her and Nick, she didn't want to carry on the way she had been. It was a startling bolt of self-discovery.

'Perhaps you were.' He touched her mouth tenderly with

his finger, his voice deep and holding a note she couldn't quite discern.

She glanced at him, her eyes narrowed against the brilliant sunlight dappling the garden as she searched his face. But before she could say anything, he turned, pulling her out of the garden and shutting the gate behind them. 'It's twelve o'clock,' he said practically. 'We've half an hour to get changed and make it to my mother's.'

'Oh, my goodness.' She hadn't realised how late it was; the time had flown. It always flew when she was with Nick.

But instead of rushing her off, he took her into his arms, kissing her hard until she relaxed against him. 'I want us to talk when we get back tonight,' he said, raising his head and stroking her mouth with his lips as he spoke. 'We can't go on like this. You realise that, don't you?'

She looked back at him and her eyes were dark with the desire he had aroused, that and the slight chill she'd felt at his words. Had he finally got tired of her? Had seeing Margaret made him realise he couldn't be bothered to deal with someone who had so many hang-ups, someone who was such an emotional mess? And then she caught the thoughts. She was doing it again, she thought wretchedly, letting the anxious, uncertain little girl out of the closet. She nodded, trying to remove any trace of her fear from her voice when she said, 'Yes, I know.'

'Good. No argument, then?'

He hadn't actually added—for a change—but the words hung in the air between them along with his smile. She tried to smile back but it was hard. 'No argument,' she said weakly.

'You're in danger of being reasonable. I shall have to bring you to the walled garden again if it has this effect on you.'

The mocking quality to his words was enough to clear

the weepy feeling and enable her to say, half joking and half meaning it, 'Don't push your luck, Nick Morgan.'

'As if. I seem to remember the last time I did that with you I nearly lost part of my face.'

She smiled sweetly. 'Don't exaggerate. I had great faith in your agility.'

'Agile I might be, but the long jump done backwards isn't exactly my forte.'

'Are you saying there's something you're *not* good at?'

They continued to spar on the walk back to the house, Nick's arm round her shoulders and his hard thigh brushing hers. She wondered what he would say if she suddenly stopped and told him that she loved him, that she knew there would never be anyone else in the world for her and that he had become the centre of her universe.

Probably nothing, she answered herself wryly as they entered the house. He'd be too busy running in the opposite direction. Like Jenny had said last night, commitment wasn't an option as far as Nick was concerned, not the for ever type anyway. Love was one thing, devotion quite another.

Once in her room, Cory changed into a sleeveless cream crêpe dress which was hand-painted with squiggles in a rich chocolate shade that matched her hair. It was the dress she'd brought with her for evenings and it was eminently suitable for a Sunday lunch at which Margaret would be present, she thought, turning this way and that in front of the mirror. Classy, understated elegance. Exactly the look she needed for today.

After making up her face very carefully to emphasise her eyes, she put her hair up in a casual knot at the back of her head, leaving a few loose tendrils about her face. Standing back, she surveyed the overall result. Cool and tasteful. She frowned. Should she had gone for warm and sexy instead? But she couldn't compete with Margaret's flamboyant colouring and lovely figure, which was on the voluptuous side in all the right places. This was her, Cory James. She would never be a Page Three girl.

She squared her shoulders, picking up her handbag. She glanced in the mirror one last time with the sort of look that said, once more into the breach, dear friends. Margaret—beloved god-daughter, brilliant lecturer and old flame—I'm forewarned this time. And forewarned meant forearmed.

Nick's mother's house turned out to be a rambling old place, beautifully furnished with some lovely antiques but the carpets were worn in places and the sofas were the type where you didn't have to worry about dropping cake crumbs. Vibrant colours, lots of big throws, magnificent paintings on the walls—some of them Catherine's own— and a general air of the house being a home rather than a showpiece. Nick had told her that his mother's success with her paintings and his father's shrewd handle on investment and financial matters meant Catherine was a very wealthy woman, but material things meant very little to her. Her dogs—seven at the last count—and cats—five—were her priority.

'Every time there's a dog or cat that stays at the sanctuary for a while because no one wants it, home it goes to join the crazy gang,' Nick said, once they had patted and fussed the sea of animals about their feet on entering the house, and had managed to go through to the garden where Catherine had decided to hold a barbecue.

'The crazy gang?' Cory was sitting with a drink in one hand and her other in Nick's as they swayed in a big swing seat under a shady parasol, Catherine opposite them in a garden chair. None of the others had arrived yet.

'That's what the children call my babies,' Catherine said with a severe look at her son. 'They're not at all crazy. One or two were a little…disturbed when they came, but plenty of love and discipline in that order soon put things right.'

'Bertie—that's the big hearthrug,' said Nick, pointing to a Bearded Collie lying by Catherine's chair, 'used to eat paper. Right, Mum? Newspapers, magazines, books, they'd all get swallowed and digested. He'd actually take a book out of the bookcase when he fancied a snack.'

'That was because he'd been left alone from when he was a puppy and he'd developed bad habits because he was bored,' Catherine said protectively. 'He soon stopped that with me.'

'That cat, there, the black one with the white paws, only walks sideways. Like a crab,' Nick continued.

'She was hit by a car and has got brain damage but apart from the walking she's fine,' Catherine said, her tone sharper.

'And the mutt with the big grin—' Nick pointed to a little shaggy dog that did look like it was grinning from ear to ear '—starts howling if it hears music. Any kind.'

'Yes, well, I don't know why he does that, I must admit,' Catherine said reluctantly. 'But I've got used to it now.'

'Mother, they're all crackers in some way or other, that's why you've got them,' Nick said with a touch of exasperation in his voice. 'Crazy gang is kind; I can think of more appropriate names to call them. Especially him.' He eyed a little Jack Russell with only three legs who nevertheless was as nimble as the others and who'd nearly had Nick over as they'd walked into the house, by scooting under his feet. 'That wasn't an accident when we first walked in, you know,' he added to Cory. 'That's his party trick. He thinks it's great fun if he can actually land you on your back.'

'He never does it to women, though, only men,' Catherine said defensively.

'Great. You're telling me he's a gentleman now?'

'I think they're all lovely,' said Cory, smiling at Nick's mother, who smiled back. 'And taking the ones who really need you is brilliant. It's exactly what I'd do if I was in a position to work at home.'

'Don't encourage her.' Nick frowned darkly and then, as a big fat tabby cat with one eye missing jumped on his lap and settled itself down, purring gently, he began absently to stroke the thick fur.

Cory caught Catherine's eye and the two women exchanged a smile.

Rosie and Geoff joined them within a few minutes, their children, Robert and Caroline, politely introducing themselves to Cory before they disappeared to the end of the garden for a game of football with their father. All the dogs joined in, one or two barking frenziedly, while most of the cats retired to the fence where they sat looking down on the antics below with consummate disinterest. It was suddenly a lot noisier.

Jenny and Rod arrived next with Pears and Peach. The two small girls were identical twins and looked angelic, great big blue eyes looking out from under shiny blonde fringes and tiny rosebud mouths widening into smiles as Cory said hallo.

'Angelic?' Jenny snorted when Cory said what she'd thought. 'Don't you believe it. They're monkeys, the pair of them. I can't let them out of my sight for a minute.'

Within seconds the din in the garden had increased tenfold and Jenny smiled at Cory over the top of her wineglass. 'See what I mean?' she said resignedly. 'They have this effect wherever they go.'

It was another half an hour before Margaret appeared,

and Cory knew instantly that the other woman had timed her entrance for maximum effect, knowing everyone would be here. She looked stunning, her hour-glass figure filling out a low-cut black linen catsuit and her red hair styled in flirty fullness about her face. Red lips and talons completed the picture of a lady who meant business.

The men were all occupied with the barbecue and the women, having brought out the salads, french bread and all the extras, were sitting having another glass of wine when Margaret walked into the garden by way of a side gate at the end of the house.

'Wow.' Jenny was sitting by the side of Cory now in the swing seat, and her eyes widened. 'Impressive. Tarty and over-the-top and totally without taste, but impressive.'

Catherine had jumped up at her god-daughter's entrance, hurrying to meet her and then escorting her to a chair and fetching her a glass of wine. Cory schooled her face into a smile as Margaret glanced her way but then, to her shock, the other woman looked straight through her.

Whether Jenny had noticed the little exchange, Cory wasn't sure, but Nick's sister's voice had a definite edge to it when she drawled, 'Won't you be a little warm in that today, Margaret? Black's not ideal when it's so hot.'

Margaret's lovely green eyes were cold as she looked at Jenny. 'I don't feel the heat.'

'Lucky old you.' Jenny grimaced. 'Still, I dare say Mum can find you an old cardigan or something if you start to burn.'

Margaret raised perfectly shaped eyebrows before turning and engaging Catherine in conversation, although Cory noticed the redhead's gaze was fixed on the men at the barbecue. Or one man in particular.

The afternoon passed pleasantly enough. They all ate too much; the children wound the dogs up more and more until

Catherine banished them into the house—the children that was, not the dogs—until they calmed down. They drank wine, glasses of homemade lemonade, which were absolutely delicious, talked, even dozed a little. It was relaxed and comfortable, or it would have been if Cory hadn't been aware of every single glance Margaret sent Nick's way. And there were plenty.

To be fair, Nick seemed quite oblivious to the other woman's concentrated attempts to get his attention. Even when the redhead managed to brush up against him several times, ostensibly while fetching more food from the barbecue, which Nick was in charge of, he barely spoke to her. He was courteous but cool, Cory noticed. And she didn't know if that was a good or bad thing. Did it speak of unfinished business? Of something bubbling away under the surface? A lover's tiff maybe?

Jenny and Rod left just after tea time to take the twins home, declaring the two little girls would need at least an hour to settle down before they could put them to bed. 'They adore being with Robert and Caroline,' Jenny said, as she hugged Cory goodbye, 'but they do get overexcited.' Then, her voice soft, she added, 'It's been lovely meeting you, Cory. You're so good for Nick. I've never seen him so happy.'

Cory stared at her, taken aback. 'Thank you.' She didn't know what else to say.

They had all wandered out to Jenny and Rod's car to wave the little family off, and once indoors Cory let the others walk through to the garden and disappeared to the downstairs cloakroom. It was as she was leaving it that she stopped dead as she heard Margaret's voice somewhere near.

'Please, Nick, you have to listen to me. I can't bear it

when we're apart. I'll come down to London, I'll do anything but I want to be with you.'

'Don't start this again, Margaret.'

'I know you don't want marriage or anything like that and I accept it. I do. We don't even have to live together if you don't want that.'

'Margaret, move on. I have.' Nick's voice was cold, flinty.

'You're not talking about that little nincompoop you've brought with you? Darling, you'll be bored with her in a month or two. I guarantee it.'

'Leave Cory out of this. I'm talking about us having nothing left, Margaret, not Cory or anyone else. Whatever you're searching for, it's not me. It never was. You've always wanted me only because I didn't fall at your feet like most men you meet. Even as a child you always had to be the centre of attention and it wears thin.'

'You wanted me once.' It sounded sulky.

'We had a few dinners, a few laughs and that was all it was,' Nick ground out stonily. 'Face it. You were between partners and so was I.'

'This is because I said I loved you, isn't it?' Margaret's voice was quivering. 'Because I wanted us to be together always. It scared you off.'

She heard Nick sigh impatiently. 'Margaret, once you went to university you found the big world of men and you never looked back. I've lost count of the number you had before, during and after your marriage. You have no idea what love is unless it's love for the reflection in the mirror. You know damn well that's true; you've as good as admitted it in your better moments. I'm a challenge, the one who won't play ball. That's all. Now, cut the heartbroken act because it doesn't wash.'

There was a screaming silence for a few seconds and

Cory found she was holding her breath. Then Margaret said, a different note to her voice now, 'We're two of a kind, Nick, you and I. You'll never settle down with one woman, just like I'll never settle down with one man. But we could at least have some fun for a while.'

'Thanks, but no thanks.'

'Because of her?' Margaret said petulantly.

'Because I don't want you. End of story. Now go and say your goodbyes to my mother like a dutiful god-daughter. I've told Rosie and Geoff to take their leave too. You may not have noticed, but mother is getting older and a weekend like this shows it up, not that she'd ever admit it.'

'I'm always around when you grow tired of little Miss Perfect. You only have to pick up the phone and call and I'll drop everything.'

'Margaret, you always drop everything when a man calls.' It was said drily, the double meaning clear, and Cory waited to see how the redhead would respond.

Surprisingly there was a reluctant giggle before Margaret murmured, 'You're a wicked man, Nick Morgan, but irresistible. I shall live in hope.'

She couldn't hear Nick's reply to this because they were moving away, presumably going into the garden. Cory stood quite still. He didn't want Margaret, at least she knew that now, but from all that had been said the redhead was his type of woman. Two of a kind, Margaret had said. The kind who didn't want emotional commitment or monogamy.

Her heart was thumping madly and she put her hand to her breast. But she had known Nick was like that all along, so why did she feel so devastated now? Just because he had let her into his life to some extent, had been tender, understanding, it didn't mean he had changed his views about anything. He wasn't a cruel or manipulative man like William had been; of course he would be gentle and sympathetic to the woman he was seeing.

She stood for a few minutes more, knowing she had to get a handle on how she was feeling before she joined the others. Then, when she really couldn't delay any longer, she lifted her head and marched out into the garden.

'Hi.' Nick rose immediately as she walked through the French doors on to the patio. He sent the Jack Russell a warning glance which made the little dog slink away under Catherine's chair. 'I was beginning to wonder if you were all right,' he said, reaching her in three long strides.

She smiled up at him, into the blue, blue eyes that had the power to make her dream impossible dreams and long for what she could never have and hadn't even known she wanted before she met him. Because with Nick she wanted it all. Commitment, marriage, babies, for ever. But it wasn't going to be. 'As you can see, I'm fine,' she said softly, loving him and knowing she had to leave him.

When she had heard Margaret confirming all her worst fears she knew she had been fooling herself. She wouldn't be able to continue seeing Nick, sleep with him, stay at his house and he at hers, and then be able to get on with her life when it finished. It would break her. This way it would be crucifying, she knew that, but at least it would end cleanly and without dragging on and turning into something which ultimately would be distasteful to him and shameful for her. She didn't want him to remember her begging him not to leave her and falling to pieces, and she would if she let this continue.

Rosie and her family took their leave shortly afterwards along with Margaret, the latter kissing Catherine's cheek, giving Nick a swift but full kiss on the lips before he could object, and smiling a tight, hard little smile at Cory.

Cory didn't smile back. 'Goodbye, Margaret,' she said politely, keeping her gaze steady and cool. After a moment or two Margaret tossed her head, muttering something about it having been nice to have met her, and without further ado left.

Cory glanced around at the remains of the barbecue and the general mess. Then she looked at Nick's mother. Catherine *did* look tired. 'Why don't I make you a nice cup of tea and then Nick and I will clean up a bit while you put your feet up?' she suggested quietly.

Catherine protested a little but not too much, which spoke volumes. Once she had fed all the dogs and cats—a major feat in itself as several were on special diets and two of the cats were diabetic—she went into the sitting room with her tea and Cory and Nick got to work.

Once they had loaded the dishwasher with the first lot of dirty dishes and utensils they set about restoring order in the garden. By the time they had cleaned the gas bar-becue, sluiced down the tables and one or two of the chairs which were sticky with lemonade spilt by the children and put all the toys in the small outhouse Catherine used for that purpose, the second dishwasher load was purring away.

While Nick washed all the animals' bowls in the deep stone sink in the utility room and put them away, Cory whipped over the surfaces in the kitchen and tidied up.

'We make a good team.' Everything finished, Nick came through to the kitchen and put his arms round her, nuzzling his face into her neck as she stood looking out of the kitchen window into the gathering twilight. A blackbird was singing at the bottom of the garden, and where the barbecue had stood before they'd wheeled it into the out-house a flock of starlings were squabbling over tasty mor-sels. Nick was used to Sundays like this, times when all the family joined together and just enjoyed being with each other. Cory felt unbearably sad.

She turned into him, laying her head against his throat for a moment but not saying anything, and his arms tightened around her. They stood together in the quiet of the old house for some time before Cory stirred, her voice husky as she said, 'We ought to go and leave your mother in peace.' It was strange, but in all their passionate times she had never felt so close to him as she had for the last few minutes.

Catherine was dozing as they entered the sitting room, an array of dogs at her feet and a cat snoozing in her lap. 'Don't get up,' Cory said, smiling. 'We'll see ourselves out.' She bent over the back of the sofa and kissed the older woman's cheek.

'You'll come again soon?' Catherine asked. 'Just the two of you for dinner so we can get to talk a little. The family *en masse* always turns into something like a chimpanzees' tea party.'

Cory kept the smile in place with some effort as the sadness increased. She would have liked to come again and get to know this woman whom she felt instinctively she could have loved. 'Thank you,' she said. 'I've so enjoyed today.' And she had, in a way.

Once they were in the car and on their way to Nick's house to pick up their things, Nick said warmly, 'That was nice of you, to suggest we stay and clear up. I appreciate it.'

'It's all right.' A terrible consuming emptiness was filling her. He had said he wanted to talk and she knew what he would say. He wanted to know how she felt about them as a couple, where she saw them going, what she envisaged happening between them in the next weeks and months.

And that was fair enough. He had a right to expect some answers from her after all these weeks.

'Is anything wrong, Cory?' He flashed her a concerned glance but she didn't respond for a moment. 'Cory?'

'You…you said you wanted to talk about things earlier,' she said flatly.

'What? Oh, yes.' His brow furrowed slightly. 'But it doesn't have to be today. We're later leaving Mum's than I expected and we've got the drive back to London. We can talk tomorrow.'

'I'd rather it be tonight.'

'You would?' They were just approaching the lane leading to his house. 'OK. Once we get in, why don't you pull your things together and put them in the car while I make some coffee. We can talk then.'

She didn't wait for him to open her door when the car pulled up in front of the house, jumping out with more speed than grace and nearly going flat on her back in the process. She saw the quizzical glance he shot her but pretended that she hadn't, rushing straight up to her room once he had opened the front door. Bundling her things into her case and clearing the bathroom of her bits and pieces, she was downstairs again in a minute or two, stowing her case into the back of the sports car as Nick had suggested.

Then she stood for a moment on the drive, staring up into one of the huge trees bordering the house. You've been here for over a century, she said silently. You've seen so much. People come and go, heartache, trials, loss. And you're still here, weathering the storms and feeling the sun on your leaves and branches in the good times. Life will go on after Nick, I know that, but nothing will be the same. And I just don't know how I'm going to bear it.

'All packed?'

He called her from the doorway and she lowered her eyes

to his. He looked very big and dark standing in the shadows dappling the house, and in the strange half-light she couldn't see the expression on his face. 'All packed,' she said, walking to join him and taking the hand he held out to her.

'Cory, what's wrong?' As they walked through to the sitting room he spoke softly. 'You were fine earlier but something has changed.'

'You were right this morning.'

'Right?' he said, puzzled.

'About us having to talk. We do.' She sank down on to one of the sofas and watched him as he poured coffee from a tall white jug into slender china mugs. He added cream and sugar to hers and passed it to her before he sat down with his own beside her. She wished he had sat opposite her. She didn't want to say what had to be said with the feel of his thigh against hers.

'So you agree we have to talk,' he said, and his voice had changed. The softness had gone and it was cool, wary. 'Why do I feel I'm not going to like this?'

'I don't think we should carry on seeing each other.' She hadn't meant to put it so baldly but really there was only one way to say it. 'I don't think it's working.'

There was absolute ringing silence for a moment. 'May I enquire why?'

'I told you at the beginning that I don't date.' She had decided in the car coming home that she wasn't going to tell him what she had overheard. He might get the idea that she was trying to blackmail him into saying something he didn't want to say, that she was hinting he let her know that he wanted her in a different way to Margaret, that he was prepared to offer more. But she would never hold him to ransom like that. She went on with the lines she'd prepared. 'The last few weeks have been good but I'm getting behind with my work and things are slipping. I… I can't have that.'

'And so I'm to be sacrificed on the altar of your career?' he said silkily.

The tone didn't fool her. The powerful body at the side of her had stiffened and tensed as she had talked on. She cleared her throat. 'I wouldn't put it quite like that.' Her voice had croaked on the last word and she took a sip of coffee to moisten her dry mouth.

'How would you put it?'

'We're different sorts of people, we want different things from life.' For the first time she could speak the truth and, unbeknown to her, her voice carried weight because of it. 'We have had something great, I admit that, but if we go on we'd lose it.'

He swore, just once, but explicitly. 'Rubbish. I don't accept that. Is all this because I told you a few home truths the other night, because I got near? Is that it? I got under your skin and it rankles.'

She put the coffee mug down on the occasional table in front of them and stood to her feet. She had to put space between them. Then she turned to face him. 'I'm sorry you think that but it's not true.'

'Neither is the garbage you're telling me.' He rose slowly without taking his eyes off her white face. 'I've held you, damn it. Felt you quivering in my arms, moaning, begging me to take you all the way. Oh, not in so many words,' he said, as she went to interrupt him, 'but your body was saying what your mouth wouldn't admit. We're not so different, Cory.'

'You're talking about sex.'

'Yes, I am,' he said with no apology in his tone, 'and it's a damn good place to start. But there's more than that between us and you know it.'

'Whatever is between us I don't want it to continue.' She stared at him, desperate, her heart breaking. She had to go through with this now; it was the only way, so why did it feel so wrong, so cruel? She hadn't expected him to look at her the way he was looking now. It made her feel so horribly guilty.

'What was all that about earlier in the walled garden then?' he said furiously, anger coming to the fore for the first time. 'When you said you were wrong about your career being your life?'

'I didn't say that exactly.'

'The hell you didn't.'

'I said *perhaps* I'd been wrong about it, but on reflection I don't think so. I've been thinking about everything this afternoon and now I know what I want.' And it's you. For ever and ever. Impossible.

'Well, bully for you.' There was a look on his face which made her want to cringe. He despised her. Hated her even.

'I... I thought you'd at least try and see it my way.'

'Sorry to disappoint you,' he said bitterly.

'Nick, I didn't want it to end like this.'

Her lip trembled but then he almost made her jump out of her skin when he barked. '*Enough*. No tears. Damn it, it'd be the last straw. Drink your coffee.'

He walked out of the room without looking at her again and she heard him go up the stairs, presumably to his room. A minute later he came back with a jacket slung over his arm and, his face set, he said, 'Are you ready to leave?'

She nodded, walking past him and then out of the house to the car. He opened the door for her and shut it once she was in her seat, striding round the bonnet with a face like thunder.

She felt herself shrinking when he joined her, the only thought in her head being, how was she going to get through the next three hours until she was home?

CHAPTER NINE

THE journey back to London was the sort of unmitigated nightmare Cory wouldn't have wished on her worst enemy—not even Margaret. At least the mood Nick was in meant that it didn't take as long as on the way down. In fact he cut a good half an hour off the time, and he hadn't driven slowly before. Cory was sure she saw at least two or three cameras flash, but she didn't mention it.

When they reached her flat he got out of the car and fetched her case from the boot, walking with her to the front door. 'I'll stand in the hall until you've gone upstairs and opened your door.'

'You don't have to.' She had been fighting the tears all the way home and her voice was a husky whisper.

'Just open the damn door.'

Cory was all fingers and thumbs with the key hindered as she was by the mist in her eyes, but eventually the door was open and she walked into the hall, Nick behind her.

'Here.' He handed her the case, his face cold.

She walked over to the stairs and then turned on the bottom step to face him. She couldn't let him go like this, she just couldn't. Her face tragic, she said, 'I'm sorry. I mean it, I'm sorry.'

'Go on up, Cory,' he said flatly.

'Nick, please—'

'What the hell do you want from me, woman?' he growled before an answering growl came from the direction of the downstairs flat.

Oh, no, please, not now. Cory cast agonised eyes towards

178

the Wards' flat just as Arnie went into full action, the sound of the big dog's savage barking horribly loud in the dead of the night. She could hear Nick swearing even above the din the German Shepherd was making, but before she could say anything the door to the flat opened and there stood Mr Ward holding on to Arnie's collar, Mrs Ward standing behind him clutching what looked like a rolling pin.

Cory saw Nick shut his eyes briefly.

'Cory, is that you?' Mr Ward peered into the hall, his eyes enormous behind the strong glasses he wore. 'Is everything all right?' he shouted.

'Everything's fine, Mr Ward.' She found she was yelling at the top of her voice to make herself heard.

'Are you sure, dear?' Mrs Ward screeched back.

'Quite sure.'

Mr Ward was now in the process of trying to drag the dog back into the flat but Arnie was having none of it. He hadn't had excitement like this for a long time.

It took both of the Wards to manouevre the dog in enough to shut their door, Mr Ward pulling with all his might and his wife getting in front of Arnie and using her ample body as a sort of battering ram. Nick stood watching them as though he couldn't believe his eyes, his arms crossed over his chest and his face dark.

They had no sooner shut their door when, above the sounds of, 'No more, Arnie!' and 'Quiet, boy, quiet! Lie down!', a timid voice above Cory said, 'Is everything all right down there?'

Cory turned round and stared into the faces of the young couple from the top flat who were hovering on her landing. 'Everything's fine,' she said again, wishing the inoffensive pair to the ends of the earth. 'Go back to bed.'

Something in her voice must have convinced them not

to prolong the discussion because they vanished immediately.

She turned back to Nick, who hadn't moved a muscle. 'I didn't want us to part like this.' She stared at him but the hard, handsome face didn't change. 'I thought we could be—'

Don't say friends.'

'Civilised. I was going to say civilised.'

'I'm not civilised where you are concerned, Cory. I thought you knew that.'

For a moment she couldn't speak.

'Go to bed.' It was toneless, final.

She opened her mouth to argue but suddenly there was so much anger in his face that she shut it again. And then she saw him visibly get his temper under control again. 'I mean it, Cory. Before I do or say something I'll regret.'

When she reached the landing and opened her door, switching on the light, Cory paused for a moment. Then she heard the front door to the building open and close. He had gone.

How long she sat on the sofa in the sitting room with her bag at her feet Cory didn't know. Eventually she rose, walking into the kitchen on legs that were shaky. She made herself a mug of milky coffee, carrying it back into the sitting room.

Her hands cupped round the warmth of the mug, her brain seemed to kick in and come to life again. They were finished. She was never going to see him again. It was over. Why had she done it, why? She had made the biggest mistake of her life.

She swayed back and forth a few times, her eyes dry now she could cry at last. Suddenly the emptiness of what she saw before her was too consuming for the relief of tears.

If she had stayed with him who knew what the future might have held? He might have grown to love her like she loved him; he *might*. Anything was possible. People could change, mellow. He could have decided at some point down the line that he wanted more than a semi-bachelor existence. Marriage, even children might have presented themselves as attractive.

She finished the coffee before standing up and beginning to pace the room, twisting her hands in front of her like a demented woman. She had burnt all her bridges tonight because Nick was a proud man and he would never forgive her for this. Even if she begged him, he wouldn't take her back now.

How could she have done it? Why had she been so stupid? It had seemed so right earlier after she had listened to him talking to Margaret, but now it seemed just as wrong. She didn't understand herself. She didn't understand herself at all. He had said he loved her. OK, it might not be the roses round the door and ring on the finger kind of emotion when he spoke about the word, but at least it had been a start. Now...

After a while she forced herself to go into the bedroom and get undressed. She had a shower, standing under the warm flow of water for some time, but nothing helped the terrible grinding pain in her heart. After brushing her teeth, she pulled on an old pair of pyjamas that had seen better days but which were fleecy and warm and climbed into bed. Half an hour later she was back in the sitting room again, not knowing what to do with herself.

She would go and see him in the morning. Eat humble pie. Crawl if necessary. She glanced at the clock. It was only three o'clock in the morning. How was she going to endure the next few hours without going mad?

The buzzer on the intercom in the hall brought her eyes widening and her heart thudding. She suddenly had a mental picture of a policeman standing at the front door with the news that Nick's car had crashed and he was dead. He had driven like one of the Formula One drivers he admired so much on the way back from Barnstaple.

She rushed to the hall, flicking the switch on the intercom with trembling hands. 'Yes, who is it?' she croaked.

'Cory?'

The relief she felt in hearing Nick's voice almost made her faint. Somehow she managed to say, 'Nick? What are you doing back here?'

'I've asked myself the same question.' It was dry and sardonic, but there was none of the furious rage of earlier. 'Can I come up?'

'What? Oh, yes, yes.' She pressed the switch to open the front door almost numbly, unable to believe he was here. That he was back. And then it suddenly swept over her. She had to tell him. This was her moment. She didn't know what had brought him back but she couldn't miss it again.

She opened the flat door, stepping out on to the landing just as he reached the top of the stairs. 'Nick!' She flung herself at him with enough force to have taken them both down the stairs if he hadn't braced himself at the last moment. 'Oh, Nick, Nick. I didn't mean it. I was stupid, crazy. I don't want us to finish, I don't.' The tears which had been on hold all night had burst forth in a torrent, her voice a wail.

She was aware of him picking her up when she continued to cling on to him like grim death, also that Arnie was barking again downstairs and the flat door above had just opened. Nick carried her into the flat, kicking the door shut behind him and walking over to the sofa, where he sat down with her on his lap. She still had her arms round his neck in a stranglehold, terrified he was going to leave before she could say what she had to say. The only trouble was, she couldn't get anything out with the tears blocking her voice and her nose streaming.

He let her sob for a minute or two against his chest before prising her arms away and reaching into his pocket for a handkerchief. After wiping her eyes, he held it to her nose. 'Blow.'

She blew, gulping and then saying, 'Nick, oh, Nick.'

'Whatever I expected, it wasn't this.' There was a thread of amusement in his voice but she didn't care. *He was here.*

'I was so stupid.' She tried desperately to stop crying but now she had started she didn't seem able to control the tears. 'And I didn't mean it. It's just that with you not wanting commitment and all that, I thought it was for the best. But it's not.'

'Slow down, love, slow down.'

Love. He had called her love. Suddenly she could see a light at the end of the tunnel again.

'What's all this about me not wanting commitment?' he asked softly, getting her to blow her nose again.

She must look a fright. Cory became aware of her tear-ravaged face and runny nose at the same time that it registered that she was wearing the most un-sexy pair of pyjamas in the world. It helped stem the tears. Shakily she said, 'I look awful; these are my oldest pyjamas. I bet none of your other girlfriends ever wore anything like this, did they?'

'Cory, none of my other girlfriends have been remotely like you,' he said very drily. 'None of them refused to have anything to do with me until I had to resort to blackmail to get a date; none of them viewed me with suspicion and downright dislike; none of them had me walking the floor at night and having cold showers like they were going out of fashion, and none of them nearly took my nose off with one of my own doors. Having said that—' he adjusted her more comfortably on his lap, stroking her hair back from her damp, blotchy face '—none of them were as sweet as honey without a trace of malice in the whole of their bodies; none of them cared about struggling families and folk who couldn't do a thing in return for them, and certainly none of them would have thought about clearing up for a tired old woman who needed to put her feet up.'

'Your mother isn't old and she would kill you for saying so,' Cory said shakily.

'A tired woman then.' He smiled at her. A heavenly smile. 'And none of them have given me the run-around like you, sending me away and then welcoming me back in a manner that took my breath away.'

She looked at him, unsure if he meant it or not.

'Now, I repeat, what's this about my not wanting commitment?' he asked softly.

'You don't. You never have.' She stared at him earnestly. 'You told me so, and when you were talking to Margaret today—' She stopped. This was what being truthful led to.

'You heard us?' He pulled her to him, kissing her hard before he said, 'There is absolutely nothing between Margaret and I; there never has been, not really. A couple of summers ago I took her for dinner a few times, to the theatre and things like that, but that was all. It didn't go any further.'

'You didn't go to bed with her?'

'I'd as soon bed the wicked witch of the west.' He kissed her again. 'That was never on the cards, not with Margaret. She knew that from the start. But she was a bit low—her own fault, there had been a divorce case in which she was named as the scarlet woman—and I provided a shoulder to cry on.'

She smiled. 'I'm glad you didn't.'

'I'm glad you're glad.' He brushed her mouth with his lips. 'And, as for me not wanting commitment, that was the bilge I talked before I met you. Don't you know that?'

She shook her head, not daring to hope he was saying what it sounded like he was saying.

He groaned. 'Look at me, woman. I'm a nervous wreck. Do you think I'd put up with what I've put up with if I wasn't head over heels in love with you? I've never waited for any woman like I have you; I've never had to,' he added wryly.

Now that she could believe. They queued up for Nick Morgan.

His mouth sought hers and he kissed her with increasing ardour, his hands moving over her body, caressing and fondling. He raised his head. 'What are these things made of?' he asked, glancing at the pyjamas with definite dislike.

'I don't know. Something woolly.'

'You won't be wearing anything like that on our honeymoon.'

'What?' Her eyes stretched wide. She couldn't have heard right.

'I'm asking you to marry me, darling Cory.' Suddenly he was deadly serious. 'I love you. I want to spend the rest of my life with you. I want to fill our house in Barnstaple with lots of little Corys and one or two Nicks. I want to make up to you for what your parents did and convince you you're loved more than you'd have dreamt possible. Every morning or our lives I want to tell you that Iadore and worship you. I want to take all the bad memories out of here—' he touched her forehead with a gentle finger '—and fill it with joy. Will you let me? Will you let me do that?'

She nodded wordlessly, incapable of uttering a sound.

'I wanted to tell you all this after we'd talked in the walled garden,' he said, 'but I was going to lead in to it slowly. The damage your parents did—' he shook his head '—I knew it would take time to diminish and I'd rushed in like a bull in a china shop. It had all happened too fast for you, hadn't it?'

His insight amazed her, especially as she hadn't looked at it that way herself. But it was true. Again she nodded. And finally she told him the words he'd been waiting to hear. 'I love you,' she said. 'With all my heart.'

'And I you, my darling. Never doubt it. You're my sun, moon and stars. Flesh of my flesh and bone of my bone. My special, funny, beautiful, incomparable Cory.'

'And you're my Nick.'

She put her arms around him and the blue eyes smiled.

They're tall, dark…and ready to marry!

If you love reading about our sensual Italian men, don't delay—look out for the next story in this great miniseries!

THE ITALIAN'S FORCED BRIDE
by Kate Walker

Alice knew Domenico would never love her back—so she left him. Now he is demanding that she return to his bed. And when he finds out she's pregnant, he might never let her go….

Available this February.

Also from this miniseries, coming up in April:
SICILIAN HUSBAND, BLACKMAILED BRIDE
by Kate Walker

www.eHarlequin.com   HPIH0207

If you love strong, commanding men—
you'll love this miniseries…

Men who can't be tamed…or so they think!

THE SICILIAN'S
MARRIAGE ARRANGEMENT
by Lucy Monroe

Hope is overjoyed when sexy Sicilian tycoon Luciano
proposes marriage. Hope is completely in love with
her gorgeous husband—until Luciano confesses
he had had no choice but to wed her….

On sale in February…buy yours today!

Brought to you by your favorite Harlequin Presents authors!

Coming in March:

WANTED: MISTRESS AND MOTHER
by Carol Marinelli,
Book #2616

REQUEST YOUR FREE BOOKS!

HARLEQUIN *Presents*®

2 FREE NOVELS PLUS 2 FREE GIFTS!

PASSION GUARANTEED SEDUCTION

YES! Please send me 2 FREE Harlequin Presents® novels and my 2 FREE gifts. After receiving them, if I don't wish to receive any more books, I can return the shipping statement marked "cancel." If I don't cancel, I will receive 6 brand-new novels every month and be billed just $3.80 per book in the U.S., or $4.47 per book in Canada, plus 25¢ shipping and handling per book and applicable taxes, if any*. That's a savings of close to 15% off the cover price! I understand that accepting the 2 free books and gifts places me under no obligation to buy anything. I can always return a shipment and cancel at any time. Even if I never buy another book from Harlequin, the two free books and gifts are mine to keep forever.

106 HDN EEXK   306 HDN EEXV

Name   (PLEASE PRINT)

Address   Apt. #

City   State/Prov.   Zip/Postal Code

Signature (if under 18, a parent or guardian must sign)

Mail to the Harlequin Reader Service®:

IN U.S.A.	IN CANADA
P.O. Box 1867	P.O. Box 609
Buffalo, NY	Fort Erie, Ontario
14240-1867	L2A 5X3

Not valid to current Harlequin Presents subscribers.

**Want to try two free books from another line?
Call 1-800-873-8635 or visit www.morefreebooks.com.**

HP06

HARLEQUIN *Presents*

Passion and Seduction Guaranteed!

**She's sexy, successful
and pregnant!**

Relax and enjoy our fabulous
series about couples whose
passion results in pregnancies…
sometimes unexpected!

Share the surprises, emotions, drama and suspense
as our parents-to-be come to terms with the prospect
of bringing a new life into the world. All will discover
that the business of making babies brings with it
the most special joy of all….

February's Arrival:

PREGNANT BY THE MILLIONAIRE

by Carole Mortimer

What happens when Hebe Johnson finds out she's
pregnant with her noncommittal boss's baby?

**Find out when you buy
your copy of this title today!**